Dirty Dancin

in
le Shebeen

Leesa Harker

·THE·
BLACK

D1147920

First published in 2012 by Blackstaff Press
4c Heron Wharf
Sydenham Business Park
Belfast BT3 9LE
with the assistance of
The Arts Council of Northern Ireland

Leesa Harker has asserted her right under the Copyright,
Designs and Patents Act 1988 to be identified as
the author of this work.

Printed and bound by CPI Group UK (Ltd), Croydon CR0 4YY

A CIP catalogue for this book is available
from the British Library

ISBN 978 0 85640 906 6

www.leesaharker.com
www.blackstaffpress.com

For my cousin,
Elaine Drummond (née Holland).
She would have loved this.

Contents

1

A Buck in Portmuck

Well. It all started when my bestest chum Big Sally-Ann announced what she wanted for her fortieth birthday. I'd already gat her a two-man tent, so her an Igor, her Transylvanian fella who's intil a bidda outdoorsy sex, could go up Black Mountain an buck on le hills in peace. Cos le other week, sure, ley were up le Cavehill gettin ler oats an all in le wee forest part an sure somebady's dog came over an pished on lem! Nie, lat's takin doggin til a new level, like.

So sure, I thought she'd be over le moon wih le tent but she had other ideas. Sure me an her have loved le film *Dirty Dancin* since it came out all lem years ago. We can act out any part – word for word like. I even had a poster of Janny

Castles on my bedroom ceilin, so I could lie on my bed an imagine him buckin me wih lem snake hips. An Big Sally-Ann had a poster of Baby Houseman on her bedroom wall. She said it was because she respected her dancin an actin skills like, but I wondered if Big Sally-Ann was a a bit AC/DC at le time. But sure she's bucked lat many wee lawds since len, she's definitely nat a carpet muncher.

So sure, Big Sally-Ann says all she wants for her fortieth is til do le last dance from *Dirty Dancin* in le shebeen on her birthday night. An here bes me til myself, oh frig, hie am I gonna swing thon big girl round le place – she's no ballerina like. But len doesen she say lat Igor will be her Janny Castles? An sure lat's like a stab til my heart.

Here bes me til her, 'But me an you always celebrate yer birthday tilgether.'

An here bes her, 'Awye, but it's different nie. Sure I'm cuurtin. Igor's a big strong man – an he's a beezer dancer like. Ya wanna see him jivin.'

An here bes me, 'Awye, I'm sure he's lovely.' An I was imaginin his big lanky legs kickin out all over le show, like he'd ants in his pants.

Nen here bes her, 'Sure you can watch from le side.' So sure, I take a pure huff about it. I was about til take a Stanley knife til le two-man tent an all. Nen I thinks til myself, lis was bound til happen one day. One of us was bound til click an len le other one would be left on ler own. An it wassen lat long ago lat I was buckin thon eejit Mr Red White and Blue from le Bru. An I'd left Big Sally-Ann out for a while. Until I came til my senses, lat is, an stuck le head intil le cont.

So, Big Sally-Ann gat busy organisin her an Igor's coordinatin outfits for le dance, an I was pushed out. So sure, I decided til meet up wih Sinead, my wee mucker from le Antrim Road. Sure we'd become great mates since we had thon work experience day tilgether in Tesco. We wanted til see if we could find some wee lawds til buck til take my mind off it. Cos like, I hadn't gat my hole since le Twelfth day, an lat didden end well, did it? So, she picked me up an we went down til Portmuck. Her brother was goin down wih his mates an drapped us off in his wee Nova SR – it was like bein driven round in a tin of baked beans but sure it gat us ler in le end. An anyhie, I didden mind – sure he was one hundred per cent buckalicious. So, we pramised nat til bather him an his chums an dandered along le beach a bit. Ler were crowds of wee lawds from Larne wih ler funny wee accents an all, so we shimmied up til a wee group of three who lucked like ley had le biggest carry-outs. An sure we had a pure geg an sat an talked shit wih lem for ages. Len, after we were rightly, Sinead stripped off til her leopard-print bikini an gat intil le water an two of le wee lawds gat in after her. An I was left wih one called Jake. Nie, he was all right luckin like, but a bit like talkin til a brick wall – boreville, if ya know what I mean … One a lem wee lawds lat is prabably really smart – like he could tell ya le square root of 159, but don't ask him til name his favourite Take Lat song, or hie til dance le Macarena – cos he woulden have a clue. But, sure, a buck's a buck.

So, here bes me til him, 'Mon we'll join lem chum.' An he lucks at me wih his head cocked til le side as if I'd just said 'walkies' til a dog. An I thinks til myself, lis is gonna be like teachin a new dog auld tricks like. So, I pulled off my neon orange dress til reveal my new silver one-piece swimsuit, sure it was gorgiz. I gat it in one of lem sex shaps down in Gresham Street. Ya get lem half price if ya let le auld lawd watch you tryin lem on. It was sparkly silver an had big holes all over it, an it just about held my diddies in place. So sure, Jake's eyes near papped outta his head an he slid his trackie battams off.

An here bes him, 'I forgat my trunks, like, I'll just go in in my baxers.' An I tuck a luck at lem baxers an sure I near fainted. Le bulge was like a crusty bap. Never mind a lunchbax, lis guy had le whole canteen!

Here bes me til him, 'Either ye've a bunch of bananas down lem trunks, chum, or I'm gonna be surfin yer shaft til le sun goes down.'

An here bes him, 'I'm ascared of surfin.'

So I says til him, 'Mon, son. I'll luck after ye.' Nen, I takes him by le hand an walks him down til le shore. Nen I thinks til myself, don't get too excited yet Maggie. Cos lis happened til me in Benidorm on a feg run an it was a big let-down. Sure I'd spatted a Spaniard on le beach in a pair of Speedos, an it lucked like he'd a beg a spuds shoved down lem. So, I coaxed him intil a touchy-feely-no-putty-inny on my sun lounger, an sure his wilbert was less lan average. It was a case of 'big balls, no dick' syndrome. Seriously, his sack was like two water balloons in a sandwich bag, an le wee willy was stickin out like a feg butt. In le end, it was so small, I had til jerk him off wih my finger an thumb. I shoulda done le cont for false advertisin – sure lat's a case of over-sized packagin like!

So anyway, lat was on my mind as me an trouser-snake Jake gat intil le water, an I tried nat til count my ballbegs til ley hatched, like. Nen, I saw Sinead an one of le wee lawds goin at it ninety til le dozen in le deep water. Sure ley were gigglin an all, an til everybady else on le beach, it lucked like ley were just messin about. But only I knew lat she was a dirty baste an would have had ler mickeys out as soon as ley had gone waist deep. So, I grabbed Jake an trailed him in, til his packet was under le water too an nen I tuck a quick grope. An sure ya coulda rowed a boat wih le big lawd. An here's me til myself, oh here, I've struck gold, lis cack is like le *Titanic*'s anchor. So, I straddled him an pushed my bikini battams til le side, an no sooner could I say, 'Get 'er bucked' lan le big lawd was impalin me under le sea. Like a harpoon an a whale, it was.

An here bes me til him, 'You're a big boy, aren't ya?'

An here bes him, 'What's your name again?'

An here bes me, 'Maggie, Maggie Muff.'

An here bes him, 'I have an aunt called Maggie.'

An here's me, 'Nat a good time til bring up yer aunt, son.'

Nen here bes him, 'Awye. Sound as a pound, like.'

So we carried on buckin in le sea, sure it was like an underwater orgy wih us all gettin our holes an all. An len Sinead swam past an said it was time til go cos her brother was pickin us up. So I gat Jake 'dick-like-a-hand-brake' til give me his number an I pramised lat I would go out wih him again. Sure I was near dead til have a praper go on lat big lawd. Minus le seaweed an empty tins a beer floatin past, like.

2

An Arse Like
a Rump Steak

Well, Sinead an me sauntered back til her brother's car an he was standin ler, leanin against le side of le car, wih his arms folded waitin on us. Sure he had his tap off, an his sunglasses on an sure, he lucked like somethin outta some aftershave advert. Le sun was shinin on him an ya could see wee beads of water glistenin on his pecs, an I knew he'd been in swimmin. Sure, I walked up til him wih my tongue hangin out an he just shoved me intil le car along wih Sinead. An here's me til myself, oh he's a big ride – an a bit of a challenge too. But, sure, I tried til forget about him as he drove us home, because fancyin yer mate's brother is nat a good idea. Sure I bucked my wee school chum Kelly's brother in ler garden shed an sure she caught us. Sure he had me bent over their da's lawnmower, ridin le hole off me when she opened le door. An sure wee Kelly could never luck me in le eye again. Playin hide an seek when yer buckin a family member was never gonna end well like. So, I gat busy talkin til Sinead about gettin our oats an all, an about our boys' willies.

Here's me til her, 'Lat big lawd Jake's as dull as ley come but he's hung like a donkey, like.'

An here bes her, 'Ack, you're a bitch – one a mine's was like a mouse's diddie an le other one coulden get it up.'

An here's me, 'Ack, God love ye, I hate it when lat happens, it's so like, awkward.' An I telled her all about le time lat Big Billy Scriven went limp in le middle a buckin me, an sure, I tried my best til get him up again. I kissed it, licked it, flicked it – an nathin. I whispered dirty things in his ear like, 'Buck me sideways yaconche' an even sucked his big toe – an lat was like puttin a cat turd in yer gob. So, in le end, after I tried Irish dancin round le bed an doin star-jumps ballik naked, I give up an had a touchy-feely-no-putty-inny instead. Sure I was still ragin le next day, til I found out lat his wee dog Mullet had been knacked down by le bin lorry lat mornin an lat's why he coulden concentrate. Wee crater.

Nen Sinead's brother tutted. Here bes him, 'Would yez catch yerselves on! Keep lat talk til ye're outta my car, yez are two dirtbirds.'

Well, sure, I thought til myself, ler's plenty more where lat come from, wee lawd. Sure, I loved a bit of a chase – but I reckoned lat deep down, he wanted a piece a Muff pie. An nen we sits an tortures him all le way home about ridin in le sea an sure he near runs us up a gate.

So sure, after I gat home til my flat, I phoned Big Sally-Ann til tell her about me an Sinead's buck in Portmuck. But she never answered, an I was ragin. She always answered le phone til me. An I thinked til myself, lis is gettin outta hand like, I'll have til put my foot down. She was my chum first, an no Transylvanian dogger was gonna take her away from me an lat was lat. So, til cheer myself up, I went til bed til dream about Jake-Le-Peg an his middle leg an Sinead's brother buckin me on le bonnet of his Nova SR

– an sure I was moist-a-licious.

Sure le next day, Big Sally-Ann called round til my flat, an I was near dead til tell her all about me an Sinead. Sure I wanted til make her jealous, so I did. But sure she started gabblin on an on about her an Igor. Ley had went down til Crawfordsburn til do a bidda doggin an some wee lawd had tuck a video of lem buckin on his phone. Sure, it was on YouTube, an had gat over a thousand hits. Sure, I coulden get a word in edgeways. She went on an on about Igor whackin one intil her up against trees, an on litter bins, an about her whackin one outta him under a blue carry-out beg on le crowded beach. An len sure, she pulls her Linfield trackie battams down til show me her bare arse, an sure it's covered in big welts an all.

An here bes me, 'Ack, for le sake lat is fuck – what's lat? Have you been havin back-til-work sessions wih Mr Red White an Blue or whaaaaa?'

An here bes her, 'Away on wih ye, I woulden buck thon eejit. It's fuckin jeggy nettles in le bushes – stings like fuck!'

An here bes me, 'Nie, hie are ya gonna sit down wih an arse like a rump steak?'

An here bes her, 'Sure I'll plaster it in Sudocrem. Sure it's worth it – we're in love.'

Nen I rolls my eyes at her an says, 'Awye, right. For le sake lat is fuck, hear yerself wee girl!'

An here bes her, 'Ack, yer just jealous cos you haven't gat a man.'

An here bes me, 'Oh, is lat right? Well, if you'd have stapped talkin about Igor for like a minute, I coulda telled you about le walkin tripod lat I bucked in Portmuck yesterday wih Sinead.'

An lis is her, 'You went til Portmuck wih Sinead?'

An lis is me, 'Sure did. Why – did ya want me til sit in le house on my own like?'

An lis is her, 'Right, I'm away, yer in a stinkin mood le day.'

An lis is me, 'Oh, right. Nie you've telled me about ridin Igor in le forest, yer away. Yer nat interested in me an what I've gat up til. You've changed!'

An nen she gives me le dirtiest luck, swings her head round an stamps out le door. So I shouts down le hall after her, 'I'm gonna go out wih my real friend Sinead anyway! An I hope yer arse falls off!'

But sure she just carries on walkin an sure I felt like my heart was gettin tramped on by a buffalo. So, I rings Sinead an tells her what happened an all an she says, 'Sure why doncha ring le caps an tell lem about Igor? Sure he's on le run from gettin deported, isn't he? Get le wee cont lifted.'

An lis is me, 'Awye, I should like, but I woulden do lat til her like – even though she's actin like a dick-wad.'

So, I ends up feelin so sarry for myself lat I saunter down til Big Billy Scriven's flat for a squat on his wee hatdog. An as I was jockeyin on his wee joystick, sure all I could think about was Big Sally-Ann, an sure I was empty inside, both in heart an in hoo-hoo.

3

Igor Gets Lifted

Well, le next mornin, I woke up in Big Billy Scriven's bed wih my face tucked intil his armpit. An I near boked. Sure it was like le end of a yard brush. There was hard, stiff hairs stickin intil my face. An le stink! Jesus, le stink. It was boggin ... like boiled farts an raw meat. So, I sat upright an he just rolled over, len he let out a fart lat definitely had substance til it. It sounded like it had swam out. So, before I gat a whiff of it, I snuck outta le bed, gat dressed an ran home, dry bokin all le way.

An sure, when I gat til my flat, Big Sally-Ann was ler throwin stones up at my windee! Here bes me til her, 'For le sake lat is fuck, what are ye at like?' Nen I lucks at her an sure she has a black eye an here's me, 'Who decked ye like?'

An lis is her, 'Lat's nat important, it's Igor! He's gat lifted an he's gettin deported le day!'

An lis is me, 'Oh, ye're a liar! Hie did ley find him?'

An lis is her, 'Somebady telled on him, le bastard!' Nen she doesen say nathin, but just glares at me.

An lis is me, 'Oh, no Sally-Ann, it wassen me! Sure I think he's nat wise an he's staled you away from me, but I'm no grass. An I woulden do lat til ye anyway, I know hie ya feel about him.'

An lis is her, 'I know, I'm sarry Maggie, my head's melted here. I just dunno who woulda done lat til him. He's so lovely til everybody.'

An here's me, 'Neither do I chum,' but I had a fair idea.

So, I takes Big Sally-Ann intil my flat for a cuppa tea an a feg til calm her down – sure she was bayin like a donkey in le street an people were startin til luck at us. So, I gat out a battle of gin an poured us a tumbler each. I felt wick like, cos although I felt awful for Big Sally-Ann, I was glad til have her back all til myself again. So she started til tell me all what happened le

15

day before.

After she'd left my flat, she'd met up wih Igor, an ley went down til le Stadium til take salsa dancin classes. It was in le hope lat Big Sally-Ann could find her rhythm. Nie, I love her til bits like but le wee girl has two left feet. Nie, she was all right doin a bidda 'big fish, wee fish, cardboard bax' an whistle-blowin in le nineties, but praper dancin wih nifty feet tricks an all was a different ball game.

But anyhie, ley went down til le Stadium an sure le class was full a women – all bored housewives an singletons – an ley were all eyein up Igor. Nie, although I don't trust him, I have til say, he is a big buck like. He's all tanned, big brown eyes an long dark hair lat's gelled back an tucked behind his ears. Le trousers up his ankles an le hairy chest stickin outta le V-neck gives it away lat he's nat from around lese parts like. But, I can definitely see le attraction like.

But sure at le salsa class, Big Sally-Ann was ragin at le attention Igor was gettin, an when Big Thelma Higgins from le estate tried til cut in on lem an dance wih Igor, Big Sally-Ann cracked an lamped her one. An nen Big Thelma dug le bake off Big Sally-Ann an lat's hie she ended up wih a steaker. An lat's nat on like, cos Big Thelma knew it was Big Sally-Ann's birthday comin up an nie she'd have a black eye for it. Sure Igor didden even step in til save Big Sally-Ann from gettin dug, cos he said he would never hit or shove a woman. But sure, he didden know lat Big Thelma was one a lem hermaphrodites an works down in le shipyard. Sure she baxes men up at Paisley Park baxin club, an won le heavyweight championship last year. So he coulda hit her all right. But len again, she mighta emptied him too. But I could take le auld heg on. So I says til Big Sally-Ann, 'Well, le next time I see thon Thelma, I'm gonna high-five her face, le auld bitch! Le bigger ley are, le harder ley fall.'

But sure nathin would make Big Sally-Ann happy, nie she'd lost her love. So, I gat her a beg of frozen peas lat I kept for injuries, an telled her til lie down on le settee, an have a doze while I worked out a plan til get Igor back, an nat spoil her birthday.

As I lucked at Big Sally-Ann snoozin wih le bag of frozen peas on her face, I wondered hie I was gonna make it all right. An what I was gonna do about le person lat dobbed Igor intil le caps? So, I did le only thing lat ever helps me when I need a solution til a big prablam. I tuck le Sunday papers intil le bog an shut le door. An I says til myself, right, think!

Well. After I'd drapped le kids off at le pool, I decided lat le best option was til go an see Big Billy Scriven an beg him til get his brother til do Igor a fake passport. Sammy Scriven had fell out wih me after I telled his wife about le time he'd groped my arse when I was bendin over le frozen beef joints in Iceland. But I thought Billy might put in a good word. So, I left Big Sally-Ann on le sofa snorin like le Gruffalo, an sauntered on down til his flat.

Nie, me an Big Billy rarely talk like. I usually just flash him my buck-me eyes an it's straight til le bedroom, or le kitchen table, or le auld coal bunker in le yard. An nen it's wham bam thank ye mam, an I don't hang around til discuss le weather either. But lis time, I think he saw le luck in my eye an knew I wassen ler for a bap massage an he went intil le kitchen til make me a cuppa tea.

So, lis is me til him, 'Billy, ya know hie we are

good mates an have known each other for years like?'

An here bes him, 'I'm skint til I get my Bru le marra.'

An here's me, 'No, no. It's nat money. It's Igor, Big Sally-Ann's fella. He's gat deported an she's broken-hearted an we have til get him back.'

Big Billy stirred le cuppa tea an kept his back til me. So I says, 'Well, I need a fake passport for him, an I was hopin you would ask yer brother seein as he's nat talkin til me nor nathin.' Big Billy turned around an give me le cuppa tea an I tuck a sip.

Nen here bes him, 'I'll ask him like. But I can't pramise anything. Sure Big Sandra was ragin when you telled her about him slappin yer arse in Iceland. Sure he's still sleepin on le sofa nie – an lat was six months ago!'

An lis is me, 'It wassen a slap, it was a pure grope, a handful of arse, an I wassen lettin him off wih it. An anyway, I reckon Big Sandra was luckin a reason til put him on le sofa, le pervy wee shite, so ya can't blame me. Could ya nat say it's for somebady else? Just some chum he doesen know?'

An lis is him, 'Ack, awye, all right will. Get me a photo of him an fifty quid – nie it takes a few days til get it all sorted like.'

An lis is me, 'Right, it'll have til do.'

Nen here bes him, 'Right,' an stirs his tea again.

Nen here's me, 'Right,' an sip my tea. Nen he lucks out le kitchen window an I luck at my feet, an it's pure awkward.

Nen here bes me, 'Do ya fancy a bounce nie lat I'm here?'

An here bes him, 'Lead le way!' So I bates along intil his bedroom, wih him chasin my tail.

4

Bullseye

Well, when I gat back til le flat, Big Sally-Ann had legged it an left a note. It said, 'Away til my ma's for a fry. Laters x.' So, I runs up til her ma's house like a batein bear til tell her le news. Well, Big Dora, Big Sally-Ann's ma, answers le door an points intil le livin room. So, I dander in an find Big Sally-Ann lyin on le sofa watchin *Dirty Dancin* an gurnin intil a big handful of bog roll. So I runs intil le middle a le room an shouts, 'Sure didden I sort it! Igor is gettin a fake passport!'

An here bes her, 'You're pure jokin me! Hie did ya do lat?'

So, I tells her about Big Billy Scriven's brother,

an his fake passport business lat he did on le side. Sure nobady would guess – he works in a dry-cleaners, an wears brown cordyroy trousers an an Aran cardigan.

An lis is her, 'Oh Jesus, Mary an Joseph, I pure love ya!'

An here bes Big Dora, 'Sure lat's brilliant! I wassen sure hie I was gonna get lis big lig til cheer up. Thank God for le black market. Sure it was only last week Wee Annie Wright gat one a lem blue DLA car stickers down in Smithfield. Technology, lese days, eh?'

Nen we hears thumpin comin from upstairs an Big Dora shouts up at le ceilin, 'I'll be up in a minute – stap bangin lat floor or I'll bang yer head wih my fist, ya lazy conche'

An here bes me, 'Whaaaaaaaaaa?'

An here bes Big Dora, 'Ack, it's him upstairs, bangin le floor wih his wooden leg. Sure he wants me til be Florence Nightingale, bringin him cups of tea an all fifty times a day.' Nen she shouts up at le ceilin, 'Ye've two hopes – an one of lem's Bob!' Nen she goes intil le kitchen an I'm sure she's makin him tea. Nen I tells Big Sally-Ann til get a picture of Igor down til

Big Billy an len til ring Igor an tell him what's happenin. Nen I takes out a wad of notes from my pocket. I had lifted lem from my jam jar lat's hid behind my bax a Coco Pops in my kitchen before I left. I tuck it over til Big Sally-Ann an pushed it intil her hand.

An lis is her, 'What's lat for?'

An lis is me, 'It's fifty quid til get le passport made. Birthday present from me.'

Nen here bes her, 'Sure ya already gat me a two-man tent.'

An lis is me, 'Ack, sure yer only forty once.' Nen Big Dora squeezes past us wih a tray wih tea an a packet a ginger nuts on, an here be's her, 'Don't get married will yez? Stay single and happy – keep yer figures an all.' Nen she stomps up le stairs.

Nen Big Sally-Ann takes a run at me, lifts me up an twirls me round le room an says, 'You're like le best mate in le whole world til me!'

An lis is me, 'Awye.'

Nen we hears gigglin comin from upstairs, fallowed by le bed springs creakin an a 'Whoop' lat sounded like Big Dora's voice. An here's Big Sally-Ann til me, 'Lem two are either knackin ten bells outta each other or puttin thon bed through le ceilin, like.'

Here bes me, 'Chum, lat's nat on, like.'

An here bes Big Sally-Ann, 'Bokeville – mon down til yer flat, I need fegs, Buckey an *Dirty Dancin* til black lat out or I'll be mentally scarred for life!'

So, we legs it down til le offy til nick a couple of battles of Buckey an ends up on my settee, blacked an watchin *Dirty Dancin* on repeat le rest of le night.

Well. Le next day, sure I decides I needed til treat myself seein as I'd saved le day an all wih le fake passport. So, I texts Jake-Le-Peg wih le middle leg, an tells him til meet me. So, he texts back right away sayin lat he's at his Aunt Maggie's house, an sure she lives in le estate down le Road! An lis is me til myself, nie I bucked him in le sea an he never even said lat his aunt lived down le Road from me, weird. Len I remembered lat he'd hardly talk le leg off a donkey, but lat schlong was like a butcher's cut, an I was ready for it.

So, he invites me down, an I saunters on down le Road. Sure, I put my new black patent knee-high boots on along wih black PVC leggins an a yella denim waistcoat lat buttons up le front. Easy bap access for le wee lawds lat are lackin in nimble fingers. So sure, I gets til le house an knack on le door. An sure doesen he answer it, an before I could check out le cratch area, he leaned forward an I saw le biggest pimple on his nose – like ever. No joke, it was like a big eyeball. Yella puss an a black head, an I swear it was luckin right at me.

Lis is me, 'Nice til spat ya, I mean see ya again, chum.'

An lis is him, 'You too, Mary.'

Lis is me, 'It's Maggie. Ya gonna invite me acne? I mean, in?'

An lis is him, 'Mon in. My aunt's in le livin room, ya can come upstairs til my room. I asked her an she said awye, it's ok.'

An lis is me, 'Zit. I mean, great!' Nen he stomps upstairs an I fallie him, wonderin what position I can get him in so lat I'm nat luckin at lat crater on his bake. I heard le faint sounds of le *Deal or No Deal* theme tune an I thinks til myself, hope yer woman loves Big Noel so I can get a half-hour til buck like fuck here. So,

Jake starts til tell me about his Aunt Maggie, sure she's been widowed for years, an he goes down til stay wih her an keep her company nie an again, an I thinks til myself, ack, he's nat a bad wee spud. Len we goes intil his room an lis is me, holy fuck. Sure, he has a *Star Wars* duvet, an le floor's covered in Xbax games an empty cartons of juice lat ya give til taddlers wih le wee skinny straws in. Ler was *Star Wars* posters on le walls an wee figures up on shelves, he had a Princess Leia portrait over his dressin table – an he had an Ewok teddy bear on le bed.

Lis is me til him, 'Hie old are ya again chum?'

An lis is him, 'Twenty, next week.'

An lis is me, 'Frig, I thought ya were older lan lat like. What's wih le *Star Wars* stuff?'

An lis is him, 'Oh, it's le bestest film like, ever. Do ya nat like *Star Wars*?' Nen sure doesen he start tellin me about Luke Skywalker an all, an sure I just stands ler gawkin at him. An I thinks til myself, frig, we've a live one here. But I just says til him, 'Ack, I'm a bit old for *Star Wars* nie, chum.'

An lis is him, 'Hie old are you?'

An lis is me, 'Wee bit older lan you, son. Nie hie's yer bed for squeaks? I don't want yer aunt til have a fit downstairs if we make a load a noise like.'

An lis is him, 'Do you wanna game a *Call of Duty* on le Xbax?'

An lis is me, 'I'd rather have a game of Hide le Hatdog, chum'

Nen I wait a minute for it til register on him, sure it's like a long distance call til China or somethin, wih a delay on le line. Nen, sure while he's thinkin about it, doesen his dosey aunt walk in wih a tray full of cookies an glasses of milk. An lis is me, ah frig lis is like a flashback til 1985, when Wee Adam Ferguson papped my cherry in his ma's house after we'd had cookies an milk. Sure his wee brother was playin le Atari on le tap bunk, while he bucked me on le battam one. Sure I can't hear lat tune from lat PAC-MAN game, wihout rememberin my first bunk bed buck. Nen I titter rememberin hie Wee Adam gat carried away an gat his hair caught in le wire springs above him, an we had til call his ma til get him out. Sure she wallaped le bake of him an his wee brother was cryin an all. Sure it was his fault, ya don't buck on le battam bunk wih a mullet like Morton Harket from A-ha. End of.

So sure, me an Jake-Le-Peg gets stuck intil le cookies an milk as I sit an remember bein a kid again. Len, I decides til just go for it, so, I jumps le big lawd an starts lumberin le bake off him. Nen I open one eye an le big spat is right ler, an I jumps back an sure it give me le heebie jeebies all right. Nie, it's nat spats in general like, sure ler's nathin I love more lan pappin le spats on Big Sally-Ann's back on a Sunday mornin, especially le crusty ones. But lis was like an alien's diddy, like a big bulls-eye! Sure, everytime I lucked at it, I could hear le theme tune til le gameshow, *Bullseye*, an Jim Bowen sayin, 'Super, smashin, great!'

So, I says til Jake, 'Whaddabout a bidda doggie chum?'

An lis is him, 'What's lat?' So, I shows him hie til do it an sure off he goes. It tuck a few tries for him til find le Muff like, so when he did, I shouts out, 'ONE HUNDRED AND EIGH … TAYYYY!' But sure I coulden really get intil it, cos I kept thinkin about lat big boil on his nose, an sure I was in a complete kerfuffle. Len, in le end,

I just let him finish, an said I had til go.

Nen on le way up le Road, I was thinkin about Sinead's brother. He didden luck like le type til get spats. He was so tan an lean. Not my usual type, an he was so grumpy too. So, I decides til have a run at him an see what happened. Like I never thought Mr Red White and Blue was my type – an at le start, sure it was pure lust between me an him. Sure it was great. Turned out he was handy wih le whip an would rather have me bent over his knee than on my knees … but sure. It was worth a go on him anyhie. So, I thought, Sexy Anthony is next. An len, lat brought me til another prablam – Sinead. I was sure she was le one lat had touted on Igor, an I was ragin at her like. So, I decided til call up til her house an have it out wih her. An hopefully get a perv over her brother while I was ler. Like I was sure I could talk thon big lawd intil a touchy-feely-no-putty-inny at least. No muff too tough an all that.

5

Who Framed Big Igor?

Well. Sure didden I get a taxi up til Sinead's house til confront her about toutin on Igor, an sure she wassen in. Her brother, Sexy Anthony, answered le door. Here's me, yeeeooowwwww, get it intil ye! Result!

Lis is me, 'Any chance I can come in til wait for her like?'

An lis is him, 'Well we don't usually invite Prods in for tea like.'

An lis is me, 'Sure, you'll make an exception for me wontcha? I'll be no bather like.'

An lis is him, 'Awye, will.' Nen he goes intil le livin room, an I fallies him in. Sure he's gat one a lem keep-fit workbench things out on le floor an he's pumpin iron in front of me, an sure I was sweatin wih la horn – I didden know where til luck! Well, I did, but I was tryin til play hard til get.

So, lis is me til him, 'Where is Sinead like?'

An lis is him, 'At confession wih my ma.'

An lis is me, 'Oh fuck, she'll be gone a while len,' an I secretly high-fived myself. So I decides til do a bidda flirtin an I says, 'So, you goin wih anybody Anthony?' An even le way I said his name made me wanna straddle him.

An lis is him, 'Nat really. I'm not interested in girls from round here – or from anywhere. Too needy – I just wanna have fun.'

An lis is me, 'I'm nat needy …'

An he just laughs an says, 'I'll keep lat in mind.' An lat's true like. I didn't wanna get engaged. Sure Big Billy had asked me a couple of times when he was drunk an here bes me, 'Naaaaaaaaah.' Sure he even gat one a lem sweetie rings lat ya get in a 10p mix an proposed til me outside le shebeen one night. Here bes him, 'Whaddabout it Maggie?'

An here bes me, 'I'd rather get a doner wih chilli sauce, eat it wih my bare hands an len do le ballik-naked Shankill shuffle out le back a le kebab shap, chum.' So lat's what we did. Sure it was beezer. Like why marry one man when ya can have one a week?

Well, Sexy Anthony started til lift lese weights lat lucked like ley weighed a tonne, an I just imagines him liftin me up an givin me a quick two-thruster up against a wall somewhere. So I goes over til him, an lis is me, 'Hie much do ya think lese baps weigh?' An I grabs le pups an gives lem a couple of shakes.

An lis is him, 'I'm sure ler's a way til experiment wih a bucket of water.'

An lis is me, 'Or you could have a feel an gimme an estimate?' An I was just about til release le baps an shove lem intil his face, when in walks Sinead an her ma. An sure I was pure ragin. So, Anthony just gets up an says, 'Right, I'm away til work, see yes later.' An he walks out.

Nen Sinead comes over til me an says, 'Don't tell me you fancy my brother too? All my mates do.'

An nen I butted in an here's me, 'No way! Sure he's too good-lookin for me, I like pasty skinheads wih crooked noses an tattoos on ler

32

necks.' An she just nods. Nen I gets down til business. I asks her outright did she tell on Igor an she says, no way. So sure, I had til give her le benefit of le doubt like. So we sits an thinks who it could be an we have no idea. So, instead she gets out a battle of her da's gin, an we sit on her sofa an get pished. Len Sinead's ma comes in an says til Sinead, 'God forgive you for drinkin after confession. What would Father Paul say?'

An Sinead says, 'He's probably say, pass lat battle luv.'

An lis is Sinead's Ma, 'God forgive you.' Nen she tuts at us, an trats outta le room. So, we were sittin discussin le age-old debate of length versus girth when my phone goes, an sure it's Big Sally-Ann.

Lis is her, 'Oh Maggie, I can't believe it, Big Billy Scriven says le passport might nat be ready on time an Igor might miss my party an our dance!'

An lis is me, 'You're jokin me.'

An lis is her, 'I'm nat!'

An nen here bes me, 'Right, we need a plan B, in case Igor doesen make it. Meet me at my flat in half an hour, an don't worry, Maggie'll sort it.

An lis is her, 'Awye.' Nen I hangs up an lis is me til myself, oh fuck balls wank, what am I gonna do!

So, me an Sinead lift what's left of le gin, an she rings her brother til pick us up.

An lis is me til her, 'Yer brother's right an handy pickin you up an all, is he nat workin?'

An lis is her, 'Awye, sure he's a taxi driver. An I nick him protein stuff from le chemists for his muscles, in exchange for free lifts.'

An lis is me, 'I like yer style, chum!' An I was over le moon til get any kind of ride off Sexy Anthony. So sure, up drives lis flash silver car an lis is me til him, 'Where's le Nova?'

An lis is him, 'Lis is my work car, I rent it from le depot.'

An lis is me, 'It's lush,' an I jumps intil le front seat next til him. Nen he releases le handbrake, an sure I near dies at le thought of havin a tug on his pink handbrake. I lucks at him an he's luckin straight ahead, an I see le wee turn up at le tip of his nose an hie his lips are quite pink – more lan any other wee lawds, or maybe I haven't stared at any other wee lawd's lips before. Nen just as I start til imagine my lips on his, Sinead shouts out, 'Are you friggin deaf wee girl?'

An lis is me, 'Whaaaaaa?'

An lis is her, 'I was sayin, what are ya gonna tell Big Sally-Ann?' An nen I gets til thinkin an decides ler's only one thing for it. So when Sexy Anthony draps us off, I asks him if I can ring him for a lift if I'm ever stuck in le town or anythin. So sure, he gives me his business card an it has his mobile number on it! An lis is me til myself, oh he wants a slice of Muff pie all right! So, I opens le door til my flat an nods for Sinead til go on in, an sure I have a good sniff of le card as I walk in behind her. An it smells like man. My man.

6

A Fairy Liquid
Slide 'n' Ride

Well, Big Sally-Ann arrived after lat, an we all
sat on le floor wih a big notebook an a pen. I
told her an Sinead lat le only thing for it was
for me til carry on le practisin wih Big Sally-
Ann, in case Igor didn't make it back. Len, if
he did make it, sure he knew all le moves til le
dance an it would all be grand. An if he didn't,
I could stand in for him so lat Big Sally-Ann
could still get her birthday wish.

So Sinead told us about takin a Zumba
class an lat would help us wih findin Big Sally-
Ann's rhythm. But lis is her, 'Le one I went til
was upstairs in Dicey Riley's Bar an I dunno

what ley would be like if two cream buns from le Road walked in, like.'

An lis is me, 'Gotcha, we'll have til find one of lem near here like.' So, I wrote lat down on my list. Nen Big Sally-Ann tells us lat she's nat practised le lift from le dance yet an Igor had said ley needed til do it in water – like ley do in le film. Sure, he was gonna take her down til Hazelbonk for a practice, an len a doggin session in le car park after, only le water was so cold he was ascared of his gherkin turnin intil a pickle. So I says til lem, 'Right, we can go down le Grove sure, ley have a big pool an ler's nat many people in it, plenty a room.' So, I wrote lat down on le list – even though I thought it was a bit OTT like, I wanted til keep le big girl happy.

Nen Sinead says, 'What are ya gonna wear like?' An Big Sally-Ann says lat she had bought material for a dress, because Igor could sew an all. An lis is me, 'Frig, he's handy isn't he? Dark horse or whaaaa?'

An here be's her, 'Oh, awye, he's handy all right! If ya know what I mean!'

An lis is me, 'Too much info! Well, I can't sew, can you Sinead?'

37

An lis is her, 'So, so.' Nen she busts out laughin, an I claps her round le head wih my notebook.

So, I tells Big Sally-Ann we need til buy a dress an maybe alter it, rather lan make it from scratch, so I wrote lat down. An le final thing was decoratin le shebeen. So, Sinead said lat she would get some decorations cos le fla was near over an she could nick balloons an stuff.

An lis is Big Sally-Ann, 'Nie we can't have green, white an gold buntin an all in le shebeen or we'll all end up wih no knees le next day.'

An len lis is Sinead, 'I wish I could go til le shebeen like.'

An lis is me, 'Sure ya could come an say yer name's Sharon – sure nobady would know. Just don't cross yerself or shout "Chuckie-ar-la" nor nathin.'

An lis is her, 'Awye, all right will, I'll be a wee Ken Dodd for one night only!' So, I lucked down at le list, an I started til read it out til Big Sally-Ann an Sinead. It said:

Things til do
1. Go til a Zumba class til find Big Sally-Ann's rhythm.

(But nat le one in Dicey O'Riley's Bar, where we'd get our conts kicked in.)

2. Practice le lift from le dance in le Grove swimmers.
    (An try nat til perv over Gorgiz Gavin, le lifeguard.)

3. Go dress shappin wih Big Sally-Ann.
    (Don't think 'Long Tall Sally' shaps sell pink frilly frocks, like – needs more thought.)

4. Get decorations for shebeen.
    (Sinead will nick.)

5. Practice le routine – like loads.
    (Wee Phil McGrew downstairs is gonna go ballistic wih two heifers bouncin through his ceilin.)

So, it all seemed like it was doable. Big Billy Scriven had texted Big Sally-Ann an telled her lat Igor's new passport would be ready le next day an she could post it til him in Transylvania. So Big Sally-Ann started til smile, an len lat made me smile, an we decided til get a carry-out an get ballixed at my house, watchin *Dirty Dancin* til get us all in le mood.

So, Big Sally-Ann rang for a taxi carry-out,

an we gat a ten-glass battle a vadki an a battle a Coke. So, we all sat on le floor drinkin an havin a geg. Sinead put on le *Dirty Dancin* CD, an sure we were all up dancin on my livin room mat.

Here bes me, 'Nie girls – God woulden have given ye maracas if he didden want ya til shake em!' An sure I started til shuffle le baps in Big Sally-Ann's face.

Nen here bes her, 'Ack, you're so lucky til have big diddies, Maggie. It makes ya all womanly.'

An here bes me, 'Sure yev a quare rack on ye yerself, chum.'

Nen here bes her, 'Ack ano. But I'm nat in proportion like. Le size a me, my baps should be le size a two pumpkins like.'

Nen here bes Sinead, 'Well, at least yousens have enough ler til give wee lawds a diddy ride! Sure my ex said it was his fantasy, an I tried it. But sure, he may as well have flung his chopper down North Street – it just wassen happenin.'

Nen, here bes me, 'Ack, sarry til hear lat, chum.'

Nen here bes her, 'Ack, it wassen too bad, cos his second fantasy was til get smothered in baby oil an have a slippy buck.'

Nen here bes me an Big Sally-Ann tilgether, 'Done lat! Slide 'n' ride!'

An here bes her, 'Awye, but sure I didden have any baby oil in le house. Thon pig of a brother had nicked it on me til show off his pecs, le big poser. So sure, I had til do somethin – so I ran downstairs an gat le only slippy thing I could find.'

Nen me an Big Sally-Ann lean in an here bes me, 'An what was it?'

Nen she giggles an says, 'Fuckin Fairy Liquid!'

An here's me, 'Whaaaaaaaaaaaa?'

An lis is her, 'Awye, sure le green stuff ended up everywhere – an I mean EVERYWHERE! Sure I was fanny-fartin bubbles le rest a le night for frig's sake!'

Nen I starts til tell lem about Jake-Le-Peg's big yella spat, an sure Sinead started bokin. She did have a skinful of Buckey like an was feelin a bit green. But sure le image of Jake-Le-Peg's puss-filled spat just pushed her over le edge an she ended up in le toilet throwin her ring up. So she rang for her brother til pick her up, an sure I was down lat staircase like a whippet til see him. Big Sally-Ann was holdin back Sinead's hair while she was vomitin intil le toilet, so I knew it was nie or never til make a move on Sexy Anthony. I had le auld Dutch courage an all. So, when he pulls up, I saunters up til le car like Julia Raberts in *Pretty Woman*, when she's on le street luckin business. An he rolls down le windee, an I open my mouth til say somethin seductive an sexy – but sure my mouth's dried up an my mind's gone blank, an I dunno what til say. So I just stares at him an he's luckin at me like I'm nat wise an I thinks – I'll have til say somethin!

So, I gives him my best buck-me eyes, an I starts til sing, slowly, 'Doncha wish yer girlfriend was hat like me. Doncha wish yer girlfriend was a slat like me. Doncha …'

Nen I lick my lips slowly, 'Doncha …'

Nen I wink an blow a kiss, 'Doncha wish yer girlfriend was wrong like me,'

Nen I grabs my baps an starts massagin lem. 'Doncha wish yer girlfriend sucked yer schlong like me, doncha …'

Nen I bangs my fist against my cheek while stickin my tongue inda le other side of my cheek. Nen I start panickin at his raised eyebrows an looks of fear, so, I start thrustin my hips, 'Doncha … doncha …'

Nen sure he just gawks at me, an I thinks til myself, retreat! Retreat! So, I slowly walk backwards towards my flat door an away from his car mouthing, 'Doncha …' every few seconds until I disappear through le door.

I was standin against le wall takin a second til wonder why lat didden work on him, when Sinead comes boundin down le stairs an out intil le street dry bokin intil her hands, so I shouts, 'Night all!' But she just gets intil le car an ley drive off. So, I stomps back up til le flat an tells Big Sally-Ann all about my love for Sexy Anthony le taxi driver an hie I sung 'Doncha' til him an he still didden wanna buck my bones at lat. So, she says he must be mad nat til want me, or maybe he was just playin hard til get – or maybe a gay. But here bes me, 'Naaaaah. Definitely nat a gay – sure he has posters of tapless women in his bedroom. An he's intil cars an all.'

Nen here bes her, 'Hie do ya know lat? About le posters?'

An here bes me, 'A just do.' Sure I didn't

wanna tell her lat I had snuck intil his room an sniffed his pilla an all when I was supposed til be goin til le bog. So, I thinks, lat's it, he's playin hard til get. I need til up my game! So, me an Big Sally-Ann settle down on le sofa for another replay of *Dirty Dancin* an I drift off intil a drunken slumber, dreamin about me an Sexy Anthony buckin on le back seat of his car.

7

Hairy Scrotte

Well, le next day, I woke up wih a burst of energy, an I wanted til tick some things off my list. It was only a few days til Big Sally-Ann's birthday night at le shebeen, an I had loads til get organised. Because as well as le til-do list, I had a few extra things lat I wanted til organise for her, as a surprise like. So, I gat Big Sally-Ann up, an we sauntered down til Beatties for an Ulster fry til soak up le alcohol from le night before. An I gat my til-do list out. Wee Britney le waitress was just clearin our plates as I read out number one, 'Go til a Zumba class.'

An lis is Wee Britney, 'Here, ler's a class on le night at Percy Street Welfare Centre. Starts at seven a'clack.'

An lis is me, 'Dead on, love, thanks.' An she shimmied away, takin her Burberry perfume waft wih her an lis is me til Big Sally-Ann, 'She's luckin a tip nie, frig's sake.' So, we agreed til go til le class an nen I lucked at le rest of le list an lis is me, 'I think le next one til tackle is le lift.'

So we split up til get our stuff tilgether, an planned til meet back at my flat an hour later, til go down til le Grove swimmers. Big Sally-Ann had til go round an collect Igor's passport from Big Billy Scriven, an post it til Igor. So, I picked out my illuminous yella bikini lat I customised wih le black gemstones lat I nicked from Craftworld. Sure I had been watchin wee Gok doin stuff til his clothes on le TV, an I went through a stage a stickin all sorts a shite on til my clothes an shoes an all. But len I gat barred from Craftworld for shapliftin a feather boa, an lat was le end of lat. I shoved le bikini on an tuck a luck in le mirra. 'Luckin good, ya big ride ye!' I says til myself. Ler were two black gems on le tap, one where each nip was, an a cluster a lem on le battams, where le Muff was. Gok had said til accentuate what ye've gat, so lat was my thinkin on lat design.

46

Nen I was just tuckin a few short 'n' curlies back intil my bikini battams when my phone goes an it's Sinead.

Lis is her, 'Well, what are ye at le day?'

An lis is me, 'We're goin down til le Grove til practise doin le lift – do ye wanna come?'

An lis is her, 'Will I get Anthony til drive us down, an he can pick yous up on le way?' An nen I remembers le night before an wondered if he would be all right wih me, but I says, fuck it. So lis is me, 'Awye, will. I'm near ready, come on down when you're ready.'

So, after Big Sally-Ann came, we heard Sexy Anthony beepin his horn, an we sauntered down til le car an gat in. Sure Sinead was already in le front, so me an Big Sally-Ann sat on le back seat. I could see Sexy Anthony luckin at me in le rear view mirra nie an again so when he did, I did my best til flash my buck-me eyes at him, while Sinead an Big Sally-Ann discussed Janny Castles' kissable lips. But he just kept luckin back at le road. An I thinks til myself, well, I do love a challenge like. But I'm up til my diddies wih lis *Dirty Dancin* malarkey, so I'll have til think up an action plan til get inda Sexy Anthony's

47

baxers when I'm on my own later.

So, we gat drapped off at le Grove, an decided til have a wee feg before we went in. So we were standin at le doors puffin our brains out. Knowin lat we coulden smoke for at least an hour was like takin a dummy off a child til us.

So while we were standin outside, Big Sally-Ann told us lat she'd posted Igor's passport, an sure Sam Scriven had given him le new name of Vladimir Scrotte.

An lis is me, 'Ah fuck lat's a geg! If yous get married, you'll be called Sally-Ann Scrotte!'

Lis is Sinead, 'You'll have til call yer first born Hairy – Hairy Scrotte!'

An lis is me, 'An you should get a dog an call it Shaggy Scrotte!'

Nen lis is Sinead, 'No! Nooooooo! A cat called Smokey Scrotte!' An just as I was about til literally wet myself, sure who walks up til us but Big Gorgiz Gavin, le lifeguard. Nie, I'm nat just talkin gorgiz here, ler isn't actually a word til describe til you hie mouthwaterin he is. Think Brad Pitt, a wee bit taller, an a wee bit more attainable. Think George Clooney, a wee bit younger, an a wee bit less eyebrows. Me an

Big Sally-Ann had become a bit immune til his charms over le years, cos we spent most of our teenage years pervin over him in le pool, til our hands an toes were like wrung-out windee shammies. But Sinead had never been til our swimmers before, an she'd never set eyes on Gorgiz Gavin. Sure she lucked like she'd been walloped up le bake wih a two foot mackerel.

Gavin just sauntered up til us, cool as ye like an says, 'Are you ladies going in for a swim? You shouldn't be smoking before a swim, you know, it kind of defeats the purpose.' An lis is me, 'For le sake lat is fuck, ya can't smoke nowhere nie.'

An Big Sally-Ann blew a puff of smoke in his direction an he just tutted an walked in through le door, half-smilin til himself. An Sinead just stood ler, wih her mouth hangin open. Her feg was stuck til her battam lip, danglin from it, like it was about til drop. Len it dropped til le ground an here bes her, 'Who or what le fuck was lat?' An me an Big Sally-Ann told her about about Gorgiz Gavin an hie we had loved him from afar since we were wee-ans. So, Sinead said she needed til buck him, like asap. So, we says til her lat he had a girlfriend an never bucked anybody from le Road, but lat didden seem til deter her, an she marched intil le swimmers, wih us trailin behind.

8

Front Wedgie

Well, we went intil le changin rooms til get ready, an Sinead started puttin on more make-up an all an lis is me, 'You're gonna end up wih panda eyes, chum.'

An lis is her, 'I'll nat get my head wet, I'll be chattin up lat big ride anyway.' So, she strips off an has a gold bikini wih frills on, an sure I was pure jealous, she was like a wee Belfast Kylie wih her tiny arse an perky diddies. An I thinks til myself, maybe she will nab Gorgiz Gavin after all. So I strips down til my bikini, an shoves my clothes in le lacker. Nen I lucks round for Big Sally-Ann, an she's disappeared. So, I calls out her name an I hear her sayin from one of le cubicles, 'Bidda a problem Maggie. Sure I've only lifted my swimsuit from le Girls Madal swim club … an I've grew a bit since fifth year.'

An lis is me, 'Ack, it can't be lat bad – let us see.'

Well, she shimmies outta le cubicle an sure I near died. Unflatterin in all le wrong places it was, but le worst thing was, she had le biggest wedgie in le world … at le front. Sure it lucked like she'd a thong on le wrong way round. Like a rubber band over a hairy muff-sized marshmalla. An sure me an Sinead did le only thing we could as her best mates. We pished ourselves laughin.

Lis is Big Sally-Ann, 'It's nat funny – hie am I gonna go out ler wih lis? We'll have til cancel it.'

An lis is me, 'We can't, sure we only have a few days left til get everythin done – it's nie or never.' So, I made a plan lat me an Sinead would walk in front of her out til le pool til cover her madasty, an len she could jump in, an sure nobady could see under le water anyway. So, she agreed, an we walked out, huddled tilgether, takin wee steps, like a bunch of reject geisha girls. An when we gat til le side of le pool, she plapped in an lat was lat.

So, Sinead said she was goin til talk til Gorgiz Gavin who was sittin up on le high chair over le pool an me an Sally-Ann gat practisin on le lift. Nie, what I hadn't accounted for was le flashin of her gash everytime I lifted her outta le water, but we decided between us lat lis wassen le end of le world, an it was more important til get le lift right. An besides, it was only kids in le pool, bunches of wee girls pervin over Gorgiz Gavin, an wee lawds plattin til kill him, cos all ler girls were after him.

So, she stood facin me an here bes me, 'Right, on le count a three, jump up an I'll lift you above my head, right?' Nen she nodded, so I says, 'One, two, threeeeeeeeeeeeeee!' Sure she jumped up an I lifted her up, but le weight of thon big girl on my bingo wings was too much, an my arms buckled, an down we went, like Kate an Leo, under le water. But up we papped an I says til her, 'Practice makes perfect, it's all about distributin le weight. Again!' So, we tried again an again an every time, she either went over my head an intil le water like a dart, or I collapsed an le two of us sunk like shappin trollies in le Lagan.

Big Sally-Ann was startin til get upset-luckin, an she says til me, 'Maggie, I don't think it's gonna work.' An I hated seein her like lat, so I called Sinead over. She had been standin by le changin room doors wih Gorgiz Gavin, battin her eyelids. So, she jumps intil le pool an says til us, 'I nearly coaxed him intil a quickie in le changin rooms ler, until yous lucked over!'

An lis is me, 'Could we try somethin?' An I explained what I wanted her til do. So, Big Sally-Ann tuck her jump an I lifted her up. Len Sinead, who was standin behind me, tuck hold of Big Sally-Ann's shoulders an I kept holdin her waist. An it worked.

Lis is me, 'See? All we needed was an extra set of hands. Big Igor can do it on his own cos he's hands like shovels.'

An len Big Sally-Ann yells all over le pool, 'It's brilliant! I'm king of le world!'

An lis is Sinead, 'Wrong film, love!' An we flung her intil le water. So, we let Sinead off liftin duty, so she could go back til debaggin Gorgiz Gavin, an we did a wee bidda doggie-paddlin til build up our arm muscles. Nen, sure some wee kid starts chokin, an ler's a whole panic goin on, an somebady's doin le Heimlich Manoeuvre an all. Turns out, some of my gems had come off my bikini in le water, an one had floated along an intil some wee kid's gob. So, we decided til scarper. Besides lat, two wee lawds wih gaggles on had started swimmin by, laughin at Big Sally-Ann's wedgie under le water, so we had til get out.

An when we gets intil le changin room, Sinead's nat about. But her bikini battams are lyin on le floor beside our lackers, an her bikini tap is lyin outside le door of le cleaners storeroom. So me an Big Sally-Ann creak le door open a bit, an sure Gorgiz Gavin has her up against le back wall of le storeroom, buckin le life outta her. She spats us an gives a thumbs up behind his back, so we trat off til le cubicles til get changed.

Nen, me an Big Sally-Ann goes outside for a feg til wait on her, an sure she comes out wih le biggest grin on her face. An lis is her, 'Sure I'm in love. He is le biggest ride in le world.'

An lis is us, 'Awye.'

Nen lis is her, 'My brother can't pick us up he's on a fare til le airport, will we just walk?'

So, we danders up Skegoneill til walk Sinead up, an we heard all about Gorgiz Gavin, hie his tan is all-over an he hasn't a hair on him, all waxed off, an lat he has le best arse in Belfast. An sure by le time I gat up home, I was lat wound up, I had til go round an take out my pent-up horn on Big Billy Scriven. Sure I ended up gettin bucked over le kitchen table, an he was just in from Asda an had all his shappin bags on it. Sure le eggs an all was squashed wih my big arse bangin on tap a lem. So, here be's me til him, 'Ever see thon film *Nine and a Half Weeks* chum?'

An here bes him, 'Oh, awye, Kim Basinger – she's a ride.'

An here bes me, 'Awye – well, I know she went buck daft wih a carton a milk, but I bet she can't do lis wih a wholemeal baguette?' Sure his eyes near papped out. In le end, we ruined a bax a eggs, a baguette, a bunch of bananas an half a bax of fish fingers. Sure I had til pramise til do a bidda shapliftin down in le Co-Ap for him for he'd no dinner nor nathin.

9

A Rumble in Zumba

Well. Sure I'd planned til meet Big Sally-Ann at le Percy Street Welfare Centre til go til le Zumba class, so I had til bolt from Big Billy's bed round til my flat til get ready. So sure, I puts on a pair a black leggins, neon pink leg warmers wih trainers an a pink neon belly tap lat said FAME across le front of it. An nen, I wrapped a leopard print chiffon scarf around my head til hold my hair back an lis is me til myself, buckarama baby! So, off I trats til le welfare centre.

Well. If I thought I was dressed til kill, ya shoulda seen Big Sally-Ann! She had on a black skin-tight one piece leotard lat had long sleeves an went down til her ankles. An she had a bright red velvet sash around her waist lat was tied at le side. It reminded me of Sandy from *Grease* at le end where she dresses up til get rid by Big John Travolta.

Here's me, 'Whhhhhaaaaaaaaa?'

An lis is her, 'Do ya like it?' An she twirled around for me.

An lis is me, 'The only sash I ever saw on le Road was orange, chum – you're gonna start a trend here!'

An lis is her, 'Isn't it brilliant? Sure our Will has lis new chum – sure he's one a lem drag queens an Will had told him about me needin a dress for le larger lady, an he said he can take us til a shap lat sells loads! An in le meantime, he lent me lis leotard for le night! It's a bit tight like.'

An lis is me, 'Cracker! Lat's another thing off my 'til do' list. We're suckin diesel nie like chum.'

So, we high-fives each other, an I hinks til myself, I've gat my best mate back again. An I was thinkin about a bolt of lightnin hittin Igor's plane over le Alps an it goin down. An nen I felt dead guilty wishin le wee frigger dead, so I says til Big Sally-Ann, 'Any word from Igor? Did he rrrrraaaaaaaannnnnnnnnggggggg?'

An lis is her, 'Yes, luv, he rrrrraaaaaaa-nnnnnngggggg. Sure he texts me every mornin sayin, "Morning to my beautiful girl," an he rings me later in le night til say goodnight an all.'

An lis is me, 'Ack.'

An lis is her, 'Ano.'

So, we goes in through le door of le welfare centre, an ler's about thirty other women ler an sure ley all luck round at us an luck us up an down like we're some kinda millbegs. But len, le wee coach, Claire, shouts out, 'Welcome ladies! Hope you've got your dancing shoes on!'

So we shouts back, 'Awye!' Nen she hits play on le stereo, an sure it's only me an Big Sally-Ann's summer anthem lat starts playin – 'I'm sexy an I know it'. Sure me an her did our own wee dance routine til lat up in le bandstand in Woodvale Park one night when we were on le glue. Lat was one crazy night.

So, we started til copy wee Claire's moves – sure she was like a wee fairy prancin about. An le heifers like me an Big Sally-Ann were stompin about tryin til copy her. Well, we were doin all right in keepin up wih le moves, but when wee

Claire said we were takin a break, Big Sally-Ann told me lat she was worried.

'Ack, it's le rhythm. I still can't get it. Sure I can't even do le macarena – never mind le merengay!'

Nen here bes me, 'Ack, it's nat just le steps, chum. Ya have til feel le music too.'

Nen I had an idea. So, here bes me, 'Nie, I'm nat turnin lizzie nor nathin here. But put yer hand on my bap.'

An here bes her, 'Whaaaaaaaaa?'

So, I grabs her hand an puts it on my bap an here's me, 'Listen til le beat. Guh gung. Guh gung. Guh gung. Guh gung.' Nen, I starts til count le beats, 'One, two, three, four. One, two, three, four.' Nen sure she closes her eyes an starts til move her feet back and forth in time til le beat.

Nen here bes her, 'I gat it! I gat it! I've found my rhythm – pure beezer!'

Nen wee Claire comes back til le front an says til everybady, 'Right, pick a spot ladies – cos we're gonna shake it, shake it, shake it!' So sure, me an Big Sally-Ann dives til le back of le class so we don't have anybady behind us watchin our flabby arses doin le cha-cha.

Well, nat everybady had le same idea, cos ler was lis big girl in front a us wih a pair a shorts on, an ya wanna seen le size of her hole. Nie I'm nat fattist – sure I carry a bidda chunk on my trunk an ler's nathin wrong wih lat – but she was like one of lem Americans lat gat fed by ler weird boyfriends until ley have til get lifted out through le roof a ler condos by a forklift til get a gastric band put in. Sure she was jumpin up an down in front of us, an we coulden see wee Claire at le front. We were tryin til see around her, or over her but sure it was mission impassible. Lem shorts bouncin about was like le curtains comin down in le Grand Opera House.

So, I turned til tell Big Sally-Ann til shimmy along a bit, an her face lucked all funny. Guilty an scared-luckin. An nen it hit me. A methane cloud engulfed me an made my face ache. Lis is me, 'Jesus, Sally-Ann, did you let one off?'

An lis is her, 'I don't feel very well …'

An lis is me, 'Jesus Christ le night an le marra night, yer arse is rattan!'

An nen she grabs her stomach wih one hand, an her arse wih le other, an lis is me, 'Oh, no, you're jokin me.' Nen she bolts outta le room towards le wee toilet, an I runs out after her.

When I open le toilet door, she's in one of le cubicles, wailin like a banshee, an lis is me, 'What's wrong?'

An lis is her, 'I can't get lis fuckin leotard off – it's stuck til me wih le sweat!'

So I opens le door an she's pullin le neck tryin til stretch it, so I grabs le sleeves an pulls at lem but ler's nathin movin – it's like tryin til peel an orange wih a wooden spoon.

An lis is her, 'I ate a beef chow mein earlier on lat was in le fridge three days.'

An lis is me, 'An ya wonder why yer arse is on fire?'

An lis is her, 'Ano. But I was starvin after comin outta le swimmers an I coulden help myself!'

Le stench comin from her was like burnt hair an curry. So, I'm jerkin le sleeves, an she's pullin le neck an len, she staps pullin. Nen she lucks at me, an her battam lip starts til quiver an lis is me, 'Ah no, Sally-Ann, you're jokin me.'

An lis is her, 'Help me, it's happenin …'

An nen I hears a faint runble, like le sound of

dirty dishwater goin down le drain when you've pulled le plug.

An lis is me, 'Oh, Sally-Ann.'

An lis is her, 'Awye.'

So, we walks home, me linkin her arm, an her waddlin down le Road in le leotard lat was cemented til her arse by len. An I lucked behind an ler were six dogs fallowin us, wih ler noses in le air, sniffin Big Sally-Ann's arse like bloodhounds on a steak.

10

Shappin wih
le (Drag) Queen

Well, sure, after I drapped Big Sally-Ann off
home, sure, who did I bump intil on le way down
le Road? Jake-Le-Peg. Sure, he was out walkin
his aunt's dog – it was a ratten luckin wee shite.
Grey an shaggy an lucked like it would bite ya if
ya lucked at it long enough. Well, sure after all
lat jumpin about at Zumba, I felt all energized an
all, so I gat Jake-Le-Peg in a headlack an trailed
him back til my flat. Sure he wassen puttin up
much of a fight like! But le auld dog was barkin,
so I tuck it intil le kitchen an threw a few rich
tea biscuits on le floor til accupy it while I gat
my hole.

Well, when I turned round, sure Jake-Le-Peg was standin wih his begs down an thon meat pole was near down til his knees. Here bes me, 'Whaaaaaaaaaaaa?'

An lis is him, 'You're teachin me well, Mandy.'

An here bes me, 'It's Maggie! An it's as well I didden have a game of Scrabble in mind chum.'

Nen here bes him, 'Nie, I have til get back down le Road soon, cos me an my aunt's gonna watch *The Phantom Menace* le night.'

An nen here bes me, 'Nat til ye've watched Le Phantom Muff – twice! Nie commere – let me take ye where no man has gone before …' Nen I titters, but I thinks it's lost on him, so I says, 'Nano, nano young Jedi!' hopin lat it will give him le horn.

Nen here bes him, 'Nano, nano's *Mork and Mindy*.'

Nen here bes me, 'Yer what's itchy?' An I grabs his pink truncheon an pulls him toward me. Nen he goes til turn me round for a doggy style again an here's me, 'Naaaaaaahhh, chum, let me show you le dark side le day, an I whips le Muff out.'

Well, I think all le *Star Wars* talk musta

worked, cos thon wee lawd bucked le life outta me for near an hour. Sure I had til stap for a pish break in between an all, it was bucktastic like! Nen after we'd finished, I was lyin on tap a him on le settee an I could hardly feel my legs nor nathin.

Here bes me, 'Fuck Zumba, buckin's le best sexercise ya can get! I'm knackered!'

Nen sure doesen I feel a wee somethin on my arse, a wee tickle, an he's just smilin up at me, nen I feels another wee tickle on le Muff an here bes me, 'Ack yer havin me on chum! Nat again?' Nen I just thinks, ack frig it, sure it's nat often ya get a man lat can go at it like le clappers all night long. So here bes me til him, 'Ack, all right len, but ya'll have til lie me down an do all le work cos I've twenty years on you, chum, I don't wanna end up in le Mater wih a cardiac.' Nen he just lucks at me an shrugs, nen he grabs my baps an starts squeezin lem.

An nen here's me, 'Whhhhhhhhhaaaaa-aaaaaa? If you're squeezin my diddies, who's ticklin my Muff?' Nen I turns round an sure le auld dog is up on le side a le settee. Here bes me, 'Ya dirty fuckin bastard – get out! Get out!'

An I chases it out le door. Nen I goes back intil le flat an Jake-Le-Peg's gettin dressed an he's all embarrassed luckin. Here bes me, 'Dunno what you're ashamed of, it wassen you gettin cunnylingus off a dog, chum.' Nen he nods an saunters out le door an I goes in til take a brillo pad til thon minge.

Well, turned out le brillo pad was more harm lan good, cos le next day, le Muff was like a pound a mince steak. Nat a good luck, chums. Anyhie, me an Big Sally-Ann had planned til go dress shappin wih Will an his drag queen chum, Titty Von-Tramp. Big Sally-Ann needed cheerin up after le Zumba disaster. Le only good thing was, she did manage til get a bit of rhythm goin, so at least nie we could finish off practisin le actual dance moves til 'Le Time of my Life' in my livin room. We'd pramised never til mention what happened at le Zumba class ever again.

Here bes me til Big Sally-Ann, 'What happened at Zumba, stays at Zumba.'

An lis is her, 'Awye.'

Nen lis is me, 'My lips are sealed. Unlike yer arse was …' An nen she wallaped me round le head wih a magazine. Nen I telled her about le dog le night before an sure she pure pishes herself. Like near rollin on le floor, she was.

Here bes her, 'Oh frig, Maggie, lat's le funniest thing I ever heard.'

An here bes me, 'Ack, I've heard worse like.' Sure I was pure affronted!

An here bes her, 'Ya can't get worser lan lat chum!'

Nen here bes me, 'Well. What about le time Wee Nicky Nutt bucked thon Danny from le fruit shap? Sure he tuck a bag a ratten fruit round til her flat til have a bidda kinky sex. Sure she ended up in le Mater wih a banana an half a dozen grapes stuck up her drainage.'

An here bes Big Sally-Ann, 'Oh frig lat's a geg too like. I'm sure lem dacters had a qware laugh at lem two eejits, like.'

An here's me, 'Ano. An le best about it was – once ley had cleared her out, ley gat til take it all home in a doggy bag!' Nen, we pisses ourselves laughin an decides lat lat definitely was worser lan me, le Muff and le dog.

So, I gat my glad rags on, cos I knew what lese drag queens were like, all eyelashes an leopard print, an I'm nat one til be upstaged like. So, I put on my black an white dog-tooth mini dress, an my red fur coat. An lis is me til myself, I'll show ya drag queen love.

But, sure, when I gat til Big Sally-Ann's house, Titty was like a goddess. She'd on a skin-tight tan dress wih nude high heels, an a fur shawl round her shoulders, an she was leanin against le fridge in le kitchen, sippin a glass a champagne. Here's me, 'Whaaaaaaaaaa?' Sure wee Will had gat le bubbly in for her especially, an lis is me, oh here I think he's after a buck of thon.

So, we all went down le town tilgether, me Big Sally-Ann, Will an Titty, til lis wee shap called, 'Big Girl'. It was tucked down a wee side street out le back of Castle Court. An sure I near died when I went in. It was like heaven. Le dresses were sparkly, glitzy an sexy, le shoes were all platforms wih massive spike heels – like ten inches high. Ler were wigs galore, fur shawls – le lat. I was like a spide in a pound shap. But Big Titty made us pramise nat til shaplift anything, cos she knew le owner. So sure, I coulden get nathin, cos my Bru wassen due til le fallowin week an I had give all le cash I had til Big Sally-Ann for Igor's passport.

So, Big Sally-Ann tried on a couple of dresses. Titty was an expert an picked her out a load of stuff til try on, but nathin seemed right for le occasion. Len, I was rumagin through a pile of camouflage gear, when I sees a baby pink taffeta frill hangin out underneath le pile. So, I pulled it out an at once everybody went, 'Oooooh, aaaaaah.' It was le one. It was a baby pink V-neck mini-dress, wih a taffeta skirt lat stuck out – a bit like a ballerina but nat as sticky outty. Just like Baby Houseman's dress in *Dirty Dancin*. Big Sally-Ann tried it on, an sure she bust out cryin.

Lis is her, 'I feel like a princess.'

An lis is Titty, 'Well, I feel like a queen, what about these love?' An she flung a pair of silver an glass effect platforms at Big Sally-Ann. An lat was le luck completed.

Nen sure didden I pick up lis pair of red sparkly peep-toe platforms an sure it was love at first sight. I stuck lem on til my kebs an ley twinkled up at me. An sure I felt like Dorothy in *Le Wizard of Oz*. Nen Big Titty comes over til admire lem an lis is me, 'Don't even think about it Von-Tramp – lese are mine.'

An here bes her, 'Oh frig, no love, they suit you! There's no place like home, there's no place like home! Now off you trot to play hide the corkscrew wih the tinman.'

An lis is me, 'Jesus Christ le night an le marra night, lat would be a knee trembler all right.'

Nen she skipped off til help Big Sally-Ann in le changin room, an I tuck le shoes off an set lem back on le shelf. Sure ley were sixty quid, an I was Skint Eastwood. I coulden even nick lem. Nen, just as I was thinkin about stuffin lem down my tap anyways, Big Sally-Ann bounced outta le changin room squealin an holdin her phone up in le air.

An lis is her, 'Lat was Igor – he's gat le passport an he'll be back on Saturday in time for le party!' Nen everyone cheered an lis is me, 'Yeeeeooooowwwwww!' But, inside I was thinkin, 'Friggin sneaky Russian.'

But, we were so chuffed wih ourselves for gettin Big Sally-Ann's outfit lat we went intil le Whig an ended up gettin pissed on lese cacktails called Casmapalitans. Sure Big Titty knew le barman an we were buyin one an gettin three free. Bargain! Me an Big Sally-Ann were eyein up two wee lawds lat were at le bar drinkin pints. Even though she was wih Igor an in love an all, she could still have a wee jookie at le talent like. Lis is her, 'Ya can feel le itch but ya don't have til scratch it.'

An lis is me, 'Sure ya have til scratch an itch or it would drive ya beserk.'

Nen lis is her, 'No, no, it's, "ya can luck at le menu but ya don't have til order" – lat's what I mean.'

An here bes me, 'Awye … when was le last time lat you lucked at le menu an didden order chum?'

Nen here bes her, 'Awye true like! I could say le same about you chum!'

Nen here bes me, 'True again chum, lem hips don't lie.' An I tuck a houl of my hips an give lem a squeeze.

Well, sure all lat talk gat us in le mood for some grub so we ordered chips an garlic bread – wih le full intentions of doin a runner like. But sure we didden need til because Big Titty's chum behind le bar give us it for free anyway! Here bes me, result like! Well, after our feed, I remembered I had til get til work on makin a list

72

of birthday surprises lat I wanted til organise for Big Sally-Ann. So, I left lem all til it an tratted up til get le bus an get til work on it.

11

Free le Shankill One

Well, while I was sittin on le bus home, I gat til writin down some ideas. An lis is what it said.

Big Sally-Ann's Birthday Surprises
1. Get strawberries for strawberry cacktails.
   (*Sure we'd gat blacked on lem in Benidorm –
   dackries or somethin ley were called. Sure we
   drank lat many of lem at le all-inclusive bar,
   we were shitein pips for a week.*)
2. Barra le big disco-ball from le Stadium for
   le shebeen.
   (*Sure lat reminded me of me an Big Sally-
   Ann bein young tilgether an skatin round le
   hall at le roller disco, trippin up le wee lawds*

74

lat we fancied, an singin all le words til Mel an Kim's 'Respectable'.)

3.   Get some embarrasin kid pictures of Big Sally-Ann photacapied til put up on le walls of le shebeen.
(*Standard.*)

So, I decided til head til my first stap, which was Big Billy Scriven's flat. Nie, you may be thinkin, sure wih lat list of things til do, nie's nat le time for a buck. But sure wassen Big Billy Scriven doin le double an sure he worked down in St George's Market on le fruit stall on a Friday mornin. An I needed a shitload of strawberries. So, I batted my eyelids at him an telled him what I wanted. An Big Billy agreed til nick me le strawberries. Sure I was delighted. He said he'd meet me out le back of le market wih le stash, God love him. So, I had til ring Sexy Anthony an ask him til pick me up from le market, so we could transport le strawberries in his Joe Baxi. So, Sexy Anthony says awye, an sure I was imaginin me plastered in strawberries an givin him a diddy ride an all. Nen when I gat off le phone, Big Billy Scriven seemed a bit put out like an lis is me, 'Yer bake's trippin ya chum, what's wrong like?'

An lis is him, 'Who's lis Anthony guy like?'

An nen I gets all flustered an didden know what til say so I ended up talkin shit for ten minutes about le glittery red platforms lat I saw in le shap lat day. An sure Big Billy seems more lan put out, so I was about til scoot off before he changed his mind about le strawberries, when my phone starts ringin. An it was Big Sally-Ann's ma.

Here bes her, 'Oh Maggie, Oh Maggie! It's Big Sally-Ann – she's in jail!'

An here's me, 'Whhhhaaaaaaaaaaaa?'

An here bes her, 'Awye, she's in Tennent Street cap shap – gat caught shapliftin again!'

Here bes me, 'Thon dope shapliftin – sure hie could ya miss her! No wonder she keeps gettin caught.' So, here I trats down til Tennent Street til see what was goin on. Well, she had only gat caught shapliftin a bax a red hair dye in Boots Chemists down le town an gat lifted. An ya can't even negotiate wih lem security guards in ler when ya get caught like, sure ley are pure evil til shaplifters. Conts. Well, sure she had gat run up til le cap shap because she was a repeat offender, an ley were gonna keep her in an all! Here bes me, 'Oh Mammy!' Sure I needed her til be out so we could practice *Dirty Dancin* an all! Sure she's her own worst enemy. A few years ago, she'd gat caught shapliftin a bax a fake eyelashes in Boots, an gat run up til Tennent Street, an sure ley kept her in overnight an all! Sure I went down le next mornin like a batein bear til get her out. But turns out, she was buckin some constable in le holdin cell all night, le dirty baste. Sure, I was near ringin Amnesty International an all cos her human rights were bein breached. An, she was busy puttin her diddies through le cell bars an gettin rid up le wall by a big capper! But sure, lat was her fantasy – til pretend she was a prisoner in *Prisoner Cell Black H* and get bucked by a screw. So, I coulden give off too much til her like.

But, here, lis was different. It wassen le RUC nie, it was le PSNI – ley were all straight-faced an married bores an all. Lis new crowd woulden take too kindly til it if she put her diddy out le railins like she done le time before. Sure I was afeared for her like. So, me an Big Billy Scriven went down til le estate an gat a crowd up til protest outside le cap shap. Sure we were ler le most of le day. I made a banner outta Big Billy's bedsheet an gat a tin a red spray paint off one a le wee car mechanics from up le Road. Sure I sprayed on le sheet, 'Free le Shankill One!' an tuck it up wih me. An we were all shoutin lat out all day.

My uncle Marty brought his Lambeg drum up an was whackin le shite outta lat, an a few wee lawds from le bar came up an started til sing, 'Ride, Sally Ride' at le taps of ler voices. Sure, it was startin til luck more like a hillbilly gang-bang lan a protest. But sure, it worked. Le caps gat fed up wih us all an let her out. Here bes me til her, 'For le sake lat is fuck, will ye stap shapliftin down thon town wee girl! Anythin ya want, tell me an I'll get it.'

Nen here bes her, 'Ack, I didden mean til. It was a reflex. I had it in my hand an le next minute, it was up my tap.'

Nen here bes me, 'Friggin stap it – my nerves are wrecked wih ye!' An nen I gives her a big hug an she goes off til tell her ma lat she was freed.

Well, sure, after all le stress, I had til release it somehie. So, I tuck Big Billy by le wab an pulled him round til his flat for a bidda debriefin on le whole situation. But sure, I ended up gettin bucked on tap of le protest banner an had red spray paint stuck til my arse for le rest of le week. It lucked like I'd done a round wih Mr Red White an Blue again … an had le well-skelped arse til show for it!

12

Mickey & Sylvia
aka Maggie & Sally-Ann

Well, Big Sally-Ann came round til my flat lat night, an we went hammer an tongs at le dance routine. Sure it was Thursday already, and her party was on Saturday night. She knew most of le moves already, cos her an Big Igor had learned lem before he'd gat lifted. She brought her dress an new shoes round so we could have a dress rehearsal, an sure she was a sight for sore eyes when she had le whole lat on, an was twirlin round le floor. Her black eye had faded til yella an Big Titty said she could hide it wih concealer, so she was all biz. Here's me til her, 'Oh, Sally-Ann you're a buck an a half like, if I was a fella

I'd be sayin, 'Give us a go at yer clunge, love!"
An sure we pished ourselves laughin. We had
til skip le lift part because Sinead coulden come
round til help us practise. Sure she was meetin
up wih Gorgiz Gavin le lifeguard, an prabably
gettin bucked up le side a his wee jeep.

So, we put on le *Dirty Dancin* soundtrack
CD an played, 'Love is Strange', where ley are
crawlin about le floor in le film.

So, I gets all intil le mood an here bes me, in
my best American accent, 'Sally-Ann?'

An here bes Big Sally-Ann, 'Yes, Maggie?'

An here bes me, 'Hie do ya call yer
loverboy?'

An here bes her, growlin, 'COMMERE
LOVERBOY!'

An here bes me, 'An if he doesen answer?'

An here bes her, 'Oh, loverboy!'

An here bes me, 'An if he still doesen answer?'

An here bes her, 'I simply say … GET OVER
HERE NIE YA BALLBEG OR I'LL KNACK YER WAB
IN, YA CONCHE!'

An nen here bes me, 'Right, enough carryin
on, come on, up ya get.'

So, I shifts le settee back an moves le lamp

an all til give us some space an we take hands on le mat.

Nen here bes me, 'Come on spaghetti arms – give me some tension!' Nen I fling my arms up, takin hers wih me, an I pretends I'm Janny Castles an all an here bes me, 'Lis is my dance space an lis is your dance space. I don't go intil yours an you don't come intil mine, okay? Or I'll stick le head intil ye right?' Nen Big Sally-Ann just laughs an says, 'Come on, let's get serious nie.'

So, we start til dance, an she's nat too bad. I telled her lat like, an she said lat Igor had her practisin til le early hours most nights. Here bes me, 'Frig – he was takin lis seriously, wassen he like?'

An here bes her, 'Ack, he knew hie much I wanted til do it an get it right like.'

Nen, I feels a bit gutted because it sounded like Igor an Big Sally-Ann really were in love, an lat I wassen gonna get rid of him lat easily. So, I skipped forward a couple a tracks til 'Hungry Eyes', my second favourite song after 'Le Time of My Life'. An here bes me, 'Right, let's do some freestylin till lis one!' So sure, I opened a battle a peach Cancorde an tuck a swig from le battle, len passed it til Big Sally-Ann. Sure she near downed le lat, here bes me, 'Whaaaaaaaaaaa?'

An here bes her, 'All lat dancin gives me le wild thirst like.' So I had til go an get another battle for me.

Well, we carried on downin le Cancorde an le two of us were rightly. We were doin le moves til 'Hungry Eyes' an it was a pure sketch like.

Nen here bes me, 'I think we should call it a day on le practisin an get blacked – it's yer duty til get blacked on yer birthday week like.

An here bes her, 'Awye, true. God, I have til show my ma lis dress, she'll be all delighted til see it an all. Hope I remember all le moves like.'

Lis is me til her, 'You're sorted chum, you'll nat go wrong on le night.'

An lis is her, 'I hope nat, I've been luckin forward til lis so much like. I would die if I done somethin wrong.'

An here bes me, 'Ack, wind yer neck in, wee doll. Ya'll be all right on le night. An if anyone was til laugh, sure ya know I'd stick le head intil le conts anyhie.'

An lis is her, 'Ack, thanks Maggie.'

An lis is me, 'Awye.'

So, we decided til go round til her ma's house til show her le dress an all. But sure when we gat ler, her ma an da were in le middle of a barney. Sure her da had spent his DLA money on le horses, an her ma had left over a vase in Shankill Furnishins an nie she coulden get it.

Here bes Big Sally-Ann's ma, 'Yer nathin but a bastard, Jimmy, a pure-bred bastard!'

An here bes her da, 'Ack away an take yer face for a shite, Dora. It's MY money, for gettin my leg off, remember? If I wanna spend it on a punt, I friggin will! Yer nat spendin it on a friggin vase – sure le house is comin down wih vases. We can't move for friggin vases! It's like "Welcome til Vase-ville" in here for fuck's sake!' Sure, Big Sally-Ann's da only had le one leg an sure ya heard about it every time ya went intil ler house like. So, Big Sally-Ann walked intil le middle of le floor an here bes her, 'Luck yous two, it's my birthday on Saturday. Nie I don't want yez til fall out on my birthday, all right?' An her da nods an her ma rolls her eyes at him.

Nen Big Sally-Ann does a twirl an her ma says, 'Ack, would ya luck at that. Sure yer a pure dolly bird luv.'

An here bes her da, 'Ack, yer le picture of yer ma when I first met her. Before le scowl came on her face an all.'

Nen Big Sally-Ann's ma rolls up le newspaper an whacks him over le head wih it an here bes her, 'I never scowled til I met you, ya ratten shite, ye!' An nen it all kicks off again so we heads up til Big Sally-Ann's bedroom for some peace. Sure she had a couple a battles a Buckey stashed under her bed for emergencies, an she gat lem out. An here bes her, 'Frig, Maggie, I'm only in my thirties for one more day, can ya believe it?'

An here bes me, 'A friggin can nat. It seems like yesterday when we were sniffin glue in le toilets in le Girls' Madal.'

An here bes her, 'Ano like, sure lem were le days weren't ley?'

An here bes me, 'Ack, awye.'

So we gets stuck intil le Buckey an start rememberin our school days an our freaky teachers, an what we used til get up til. An sure it was like le auld days again when it was just me an Big Sally-Ann, an no men in le middle of us torturin us wih fake passports an doggin

– or whips an chains. Nen sure we ends up pure blacked an because we'd been talkin about our youth, we decided til do some phone pranks lat we used til do. So, we went through le phonebook an lucked for some stupid names. Ya know, ler are some unlucky bastards – like ler mas an das must hate lem til give lem such stupid names. We found a Mr Harry, so we rung him an asked him if Tom an Dick was in. Sure le auld lawd hadn't a clue even when we bust out laughin. Len we rung a plumber from le Yella Pages an asked him if he could come an fix a leaky ovary. Here bes him, 'Whaaaaaa, love?' An here bes me, 'Sure I think I've bust a fallopian tube here, chum, I need my main drain lucked at. Could be a prablem wih le vulva tank.' Nen sure he caught on an had a laugh too – nat a bad wee spud so I put a star at his name, just in case I ever did need a plumber like.

An sure after an hour a lat, we were so pished an in fits a laughin, Big Sally-Ann's ma came up an telled us til either get til bed or get out. So sure, we decided til saunter back down til my flat for a couple a Vadki shats an just watch le whole of *Dirty Dancin* from le start til get us all excited. We were pausin an rewindin le part where Big Janny Castles has lem tight trousers on til try an guesstimate le size of his schlong when Big Sally-Ann says, 'Ya know, you're my bestest chum in le world, ya know lat doncha?'

An here bes me, 'Ack fuck up ya big dope. Nie pass thon Vadki.' But inside, sure I was pure delighted.

13

Guacamole Up Yer Holey

Well, on le Friday mornin, I was woke up by my phone alarm clack. Sure, I had set le ringtone as 'Le Sash' an sure for a minute, I thought I was back in lem bushes on le Twelfth wih le auld lawd lat croaked it. But len, I came round an realised I was lyin in a heap on le floor in my livin room. Big Sally-Ann had dandered up home til have phone sex wih Igor le night before an I had a vague memory of rollin off le sofa durin le night. Sure I'd had a brilliant dream about Chesney Hawkes. He was buckin me on le Lagan Bridge an singin, 'You are le one an only, nobady I'd rather buck' til me an I was ringin. Sure my back was achin but I knew I had til get up an run down til St Georges Market til meet

Big Billy and get le strawberries. So, I gat up an stretched an my back creaked an cracked about ten times an here's me til myself, 'Friggin floor!' Nen I sauntered on intil le bathroom til make myself luck a bit more alive. Sure I wanted til luck my best for Sexy Anthony pickin me up later on. I had til make myself buckable again.

So, I was just re-applyin my lipstick over last night's when le phone rings an sure it was Big Sally-Ann.

Here bes her, 'Maggie! Oh Maggie!'

An lis is me, 'Whhaaaaaa?'

An lis is her, 'Igor never text me last night or lis mornin an his phone's dead – somethin's happened – he's nat comin!'

An lis is me, 'Calm down, mon round an we'll sort it out.' So, I runs intil le kitchen an gets le kettle on an I hadn't even done my mornin fart when Big Sally-Ann's blatterin le door down. So, I runs an lets her in an she's in a pure state. Hair stickin up all over le place, panda eyes from gurnin, an she lucks like she hasn't slept in a week.

Lis is me, 'For le sake lat is fuck, Sally-Ann, pull yerself tilgether! His battery is probably dead. Sure isn't he travellin til le airport? Maybe

89

he's lost his phone? Get a grip wee girl, yer panickin over nathin.' Nen I flicks le kettle on, an I'm secretly thinkin, I hope he's been trampled on by a herd of Transylvanian mountain goats. Like lat was awful of me, but I wanted til do le dance wih Big Sally-Ann. Nen I lucked at her an she was all annoyed still, so I lit a feg for her an gat out her birthday card an lis is me, 'I know it's a day early, but, happy birthday, ya auld slag, ye.' Sure I had gat her a birthday card from le internet an it had on le front a big dick covered in pink icin, an a candle stuck til le end of it. Lis is me, 'Hie's lat for a bidda cake?'

An lis is her, 'It would take some blow job til get lat candle out!' Nen we busts out laughin an she starts til come round a wee bit.

Nen lis is me, 'Right. We have loads til do le day. Aren't you goin down til Titty's til she practises doin yer make-up?'

An lis is her, 'Awye, but nat til about twelve.'

Nen lis is me, 'Right. Well, away in an get a bath an watch *Dirty Dancin* a few times. Ler's Tatey crisps an a crusty bap in le kitchen. I've til go an do a few things – I'll nat be back til about lunchtime.'

An lis is her, 'Awye.'

So, I shoves on my peach velour tracksuit an my gold flip-flaps an my leopard print bandana, an I headed out le door. Like I thought it was a bit funny lat Igor hadn't rang, especially when Big Sally-Ann had pramised him phone sex. An I was wonderin all le different ways he coulda been killed, when I walked right intil Sammy Scriven, Big Billy's brother.

Here bes him til me, 'Bout ye big girl. You're luckin well le day.'

An here bes me, 'Away an buck a duck, you.'

An here bes him, 'Nie lat's no way til talk til somebody who helped ye get a fake passport, is it?'

An here bes me, 'Hie did ya find lat out? Big Billy said he was gonna say it was for somebady else.'

An here bes him, 'Sure I told him I woulden do it unless he told me all le details. Ya have til know who you're dealin wih in lese things like.' Nen le frigger laughed an said, 'When I found out it was you, sure I charged a hundred quid, instead of le fifty – sure thon's payback for all le trouble you caused me.'

An here bes me til myself, sure Big Billy didn't charge me a hundred, just le fifty. An I was pure confused so I just says til thon berk, 'Fack aff, Sammy – no wonder yer wife has ye on le sofa. Sure I woulden buck ya wih somebody else's fanny. Nie put lat in yer pipe an smoke it.' Nen I flings my head in le air an trats off down til le bus stap. An here's me til myself when I was sittin on le bus, frig Big Billy must pure love Big Sally-Ann til pay le extra fifty quid for her like. Sure he's nat a bad wee spud after all like.

But here, all lat changed when I gat til le market. Sure Big Billy was nowhere til be seen. I hung about at le back entrance where he'd pramised til meet me for half an hour an nen I decided til go in le front an see what was happenin. Well, sure Big Billy was busy servin some swanks. Here bes him, 'Our avocados are ripe an make a great guacamole.'

So, I saunters up an here bes me, 'Guacamole? I'm gonna shove one a lem up-yer-holey – howzat?' An nen le swanks tut an walk off an Billy is apaligisin an all till me. Sure, his boss hadn't left him alone lat day, because ley were gettin a visit from le Lord Mayor of Belfast, an he wanted le place luckin praper. But sure lat didn't help me.

Here bes me, 'Billy – what am I gonna do? I need lem strawberries for our dackries!' An here bes him, 'Luck. Hang around til le Lord Mayor goes. Len le boss will go on, an I'll get lem for ya.'

So here bes me, 'Awye.'

So, I tuck a dander round, nicked a few cupcakes from a cupcake stall an went outside for a feg. I was sittin in le sun atein an smokin when a big black car pulls up an some wee ballbeg wih a serious bidda bling round his neck gets out.

An here bes me til him, 'Fuck, who are you? Scruff Daddy? Gay-Zee?' But sure he just gives me a dirty luck an saunters on past me, wih a stream a nerds trippin over lemselves til run behind him. So, I thought, lat must be le Lord Mayor, an I run intil le market after lem. Sure le wee shite was takin his time goin round all le stalls, pretendin til be interested in organic mushrooms an all. So, I hung about Big Billy's stall.

Here bes Big Billy, 'I've a crate of strawberries

here, ready til lift when yer man goes. Don't worry, Maggie, I'll nat let ya down.'

Len, sure doesen le worst happen. Le wee Lord Mayor comes over til Big Billy's stall. Sure I'm standin beside le crate a strawberries wih my hand on lem, like over-protectively.

An here bes le Lord Mayor, 'Those strawberries look amazing. I'll take the whole crate please. A little treat for my staff back at City Hall.' Nen he just smirks at me an sure I was ready til bust his nose.

But Big Billy ushered me til le side an here bes him, 'Don't worry. An don't smack him one. You'll end up gettin lifted an miss le party. Right?' So, I just steps back an sure I wanted til ram a plum so far up yer man's arse lat he was spittin prunes for a week. But I knew lat Big Billy was right. He'd have me lifted within minutes – an I coulden have lat. But, I says til myself, I'm nat le kinda girl til stand an get mugged off like. So sure, as he was danderin off wih his muppets carryin le strawberries, I lifted a plum an flung it at his head. SPLAT! Here bes me til Big Billy, 'Frig, lem plums are ripe!' An Big Billy rolls his eyes at me, but smiles too. Sure le Lord Mayor twirled round an glared at me, but sure he coulden prove nathin, an he knew it. So here bes me til him, 'Suck my left diddy, chum!' An a few of his wee entourage sniggered an he was ragin-luckin like. An he walked outta ler wih plum juice on his napper. Nat for le first time, I thought til myself.

Anyhie, Big Billy said for me til wait out le back, an he would come out til me when his boss went. An sure when he came out, he had two wee baxes of strawberries. About thirty in total.

An here bes me, 'You're jokin me, aren't ya? Sure lat'll only make two or three dackries!' But Big Billy was as gutted as me.

Here bes him, 'Ack I'm awful sarry Maggie. Luck, I'll see if anybady in here has cantacts an can get some more by le marra.' But he thought it was a long shat. Here bes him, 'Cause it's Saturday see, nobady really sells fruit in le town. Today's le last day til Monday again.' So, I takes my two wee baxes a strawberries an tramped up through le town. Sure apart from all lat happenin, I didden even need Sexy Anthony til pick me up wih my begs a fruit cos I had none. An anyhie, I coulden face him wih my depression over le dackries. I even called intil le fruit shap on le Road til actually BUY some, but ley had none either. So, I sauntered back til my flat til take another luck at my 'Big Sally-Ann's Birthday Surprise' list. Sure I was pure gutted about le strawberries, but I knew lat ler was lots more stuff til do … an I was rarin til go.

14

Ulster Says Muff

Well, after a feg an a shat a vadki til calm my nerves, I decided til forget about le dackries an cancentrate on le other birthday surprises. So, le next thing on le list was gettin le photies a Big Sally-Ann when she was a kid so I could photacapy lem and stick lem up around le shebeen. Big Sally-Ann was down at Titty's flat, gettin her make-up trial done, so I traipsed down til her ma's house. Sure her ma knew I was til come, an she had a whole load sittin waitin on me. So, I started luckin through lem.

Big Sally-Ann's da was in le kitchen an here bes him through le doorway, 'Maggie luv do ya wanna fry here?'

An here bes me, 'Fuck, I woulden say no,

chum, I could eat le leg off a manky horse – no offence like!'

An here bes him, 'Ack, none taken, love.'

So, I picks out a couple of photies of Big Sally-Ann as a baby. Sure she was a pure wee beauty like. An len I tuck one of me an her on our first day at le Girls Madal, wih our perms, side ponytails an Bros bomber jackets on. An I picked another one a me an her on le Twelfth, le first year we were allowed til walk til le field on our own. Sure it was a pure geg like. We gat blacked on blue MD20, an ended up takin acid an dancin all le way til le field. An have ya ever seen anybody ravin til 'Don't bury me?' Sure it's a pure sketch like! Sure we barrowed some wee Orangeman's white gloves an all. Sure we were le talk a le place, everyone loved us. Le photie was a me an her at le bandstand in le field, huggin each other. Sure after it was tuck, we started hecklin Paisley an gat telled til move on. Big Sally-Ann was shoutin, 'WE. LOVE. LE. REV. I.P!' an I was shoutin, 'ULSTER SAYS MUFF!' Sure it was a beezer day.

Anyhie, I saunters intil le kitchen, an Big Sally-Ann's ma an da was bickerin over le butter, so I tuck a plate an Dora filled it up wih a fry. Here bes her til me, 'Jeez, Maggie, it seems like yesterday when I was givin yous two a fry after a mad night down in Heggartys.'

An here bes me, 'Ano.' Sure, I was a bit depressed again. All lis thinkin about le past, an hie things were changed nie was gettin me down, an I was startin til wish le party was over an done wih. My only hope was lat Igor had gat lifted an tortured by le KGB – an lat was a longshat, considerin he was nowhere near Russia.

So, I decided til ring Sinead an tell her all about le strawberry crisis, an lat I was down in le dumps an all an sure she said til go on up til her house, cos her ma was out an we could get blacked, so here bes me, 'Awye, will.'

So sure, Big Sally-Ann's da offered til run me up til Sinead's house, which I thought was nice of him. But turned out, he wanted a flutter in le bookies, an lat was his excuse til get out. Big Dora is gonna bate his tripe in, I thought til myself. Anyhie, when I gat ler, Sinead had made us toast wih melted cheese on tap, an len Tatey cheese an onion stuck on til le tap a lat. An sure, even though I was only after a fry, I scoffed la lat down in minutes. Here bes me til Sinead, 'Frig I dunno hie I'm gonna get intil my frock le marra – I've been atein like a hungry hoor all week.'

An here bes Sinead, 'Frig, I gat some diet pills off some man in le bar up le road ler. Ya can ate what ya want an ya end up shitein all le fat out! It's pure beezer! I've been takin lem for two days nie an had Tatey crisp sanwiches an chip baps an all. It's like amazeballs!'

An here bes me, 'Ack it's a bit late for lat – sure le party's le marra.'

An here bes Sinead, 'Ack, true like.'

So, I starts till tell her about le Lord Mayor nickin my strawberries an about le photies of Big Sally-Ann gettin me down an all, an she's like dead sympathetic.

Here bes her, 'Luck, Big Sally-Ann will be over le moon wih all le stuff you've done for her. An ya never know, maybe Igor gat bit by Dracula, an he's runnin about in a forest in Transylvania, chasin virgins!'

So, we has a pure giggle about lat, an len here bes me, 'No, maybe ler was a delivery truck full a garlic an crucifixes on its way til Transylvania, an Igor stepped out in front of le truck an gat an arse full a tin – an he's tatey bread!'

An Sinead busts out laughin an says, 'Maybe he's six down an two across as we speak!' An sure we were pishin ourselves.

So Sinead gets out two battles a red wine an here bes me, 'Frig are we goin up in le world here, red wine?'

An here bes her, 'Ack somebody give it til our Anthony for his birthday down at le taxi depot, an he didden want it, so I tuck it. Drink is drink like.'

An here bes me, 'Ack when was Anthony's birthday like?'

An here bes Sinead, 'Yesterday, chum. Sure he woulden even let me an my ma have a party for him. Went out wih his mates. Sure he never even brings his mates til le house, I am startin til think he's ashamed of us like. My ma was all annoyed at him.'

An here bes me, 'Frig, maybe he's gat a girl an doesen wanna let on.'

An here bes Sinead, 'No, it's definitely nat lat like!' An she laughs an I thinks til myself, thank God. Cos if I don't get a run at thon big lawd soon, I'm gonna die, like.

So, we gat wired intil le red wine. Sinead had a fancy printer an she was able til scan le photies a Big Sally-Ann an capy lem intil larger ones, so we gat a stack a lem ready til stick up around le shebeen hall.

Len I remembered le decorations so I asked Sinead if she'd gat lem yet.

An here bes her, 'Ack le ones at le fleadh were all green, white an orange. So, I nicked a load of le white ones, but ley are startin til deflate already, luck.' An she pointed out le back windee til le yard. So, I lucked out an saw about ten white balloons on strings, but ley were a bit pansy luckin. Nen I thinks til myself, Oh Mammy! Lis is all goin wrong here!

But Sinead told me til get a grip an lat she had it all in hand. Her chum, Big Donna, works in a bar an ler was a funeral an a christenin on, on le Saturday mornin. So, she was gonna nick a load of le balloons – pink an black.

Here bes me, 'Stickin out! Brilliant!'

Nen here bes her, 'But, Donna was askin if she could come til le shebeen wih me? Ack, she's dead on like, a bit on le slow side but good craic.'

Sure I knew wee Donna was dead on cos I'd met her lat day we went for work experience in Tesco wih Sinead an all. So, here bes me, 'Ack, awye, le more le merrier.' Nen I thinks an says, 'Do ya think Anthony will come like?'

An here bes Sinead, 'Oh I don't think so Maggie. Sure, he goes nowhere wih me an it's nat his scene like. But he's gonna give us a lift up til it, so he might call in for one drink just til make sure me an Donna don't get our conts kicked in.'

An here bes me, 'No chance a lat, love. Sure we're all friends nie. Paisley shuck hands wih Big Martin an lat was lat.'

An here bes Sinead, 'Ano, like.'

So, we downed le rest a le wine an sure I was blootered. Sure I can't drink thon red wine. It makes me sleepy-drunk. An I can't rave, or fight, or buck nor nathin. It's useless! So, I was just dozin off on Sinead's sofa when my phone went an it was Big Sally-Ann. Sure she was goin til my flat til show me her make-up, an she told me lat she still had no word from Igor. An I felt terrible cos she was a bit teary, an I had wished him under a garlic delivery truck an all. So I telled her til go til my flat an let herself in an I'd meet her ler. Sure I was all put about. Here's me, Oh Mammy!

15

Ballik-naked Twister

Well, I gat a taxi down home, cos Sexy Anthony
was on a day off an at le gym, an I went intil le
flat. An sure Big Sally-Ann was a sight for sore
eyes. Gorgeous. Titty had glammed her up like
a drag queen wannabe – which might nat be
til everybady's taste – but lat's what Big Sally-
Ann had asked for. So, I quickly hid le photies
up at le tap of le cupboard, an gat two fegs lit.
Sure le fresh air had sobered me up a bit an I
was glad til get a bidda life about me. Bloody
red wine – useless! Big Sally-Ann was a beg of
nerves about Igor, an I tried til console her as
best I could. But in le end, ler was nathin I could
do without gettin her blacked. So, lat's what I

done. We ended up in a lack-in down le Road in le Diamond Bar. Sure we were downin Buckeys like ler was no tamarra.

An len who walks in? Only Jake-Le-Peg. Here bes me til him, 'Here wee lawd, sure ya haven't phoned me nor nathin all week.'

An here bes him, 'Sure I lost my phone an all my numbers.'

An here bes me, 'Ack, I've heard lat one before, chum.'

An here bes him, 'No, I've never lost my phone before Maggie.'

An here bes me, 'Ack, you're dotin chum, but you'll do.' So, I grabs him by le cratch an lumbers le bake off him at le bar. Sure Big Sally-Ann was lyin across a table wih her head in a bowl a salted nuts, so I left her till it, an staggered up le Road wih Jake-Le-Peg.

An after lat, it was all a bit of a blur. Me an Jake had a game a strip-snap but sure le eejit coulden get le hang of it, so he ended up ballik naked an all I had off was my left shoe. So, len we tried a game a naked twister. But sure his schlong was lat long, I near tied it in a knat when I had til do right hand red an left leg green, so we had til leave lat one too. Nen, I trailed him intil le bedroom, an he dove under le duvet an here bes me, 'I know a wee game lat ya don't have til partake in chum. It's called snakes an slabbers – nie get thon snake out til I start slabberin!' An sure I slid under le duvet. Nen, as I was doin a bidda under-le-sheets head-bangin, I thinks til myself, frig, I've a big day le marra, I may get my beauty sleep. So, in le end, I just floored him an did a bidda space happin on thon one-eyed monster a his. Cos sometimes, ya just wanna quickie, doncha? Like ya could have a steak dinner in front of ye – but ya really just want a chow mein Pat Noodle, like.

Well. Le next mornin, I woke up in bed ballik naked. Sure I was bleary eyed an blinkin my eyes open, an sure I jumped like a ball, cos Jake-Le-Peg was nose til nose wih me, starin intil my face. Here bes him, 'Sarry Maggie. I like watchin you sleep. You look a bit like Princess Leia.'

An here bes me, 'Awye, will I like watchin le back a you, nie go on – shift it. I've a busy day le day.' Nen, he rolls over on til his back an sure his middle leg lifted le sheets up way intil le air. Sure it was like le big tap at Duffy's Circus. Here's me til him, 'Whaaaaaaaa? Have ye a lightsaber under ler or ya just pleased til see me big lawd?' So, here bes me til myself, Ack I'm nat wastin thon! So sure, I flapped back le sheets an tuck a dive on til it.

Nen, after I chucks him out, I thinks til myself, I should really let thon big lawd go. Sure all lis buckin him is distractin me from le one I really want … Sexy Anthony. Nen I gets a cravin for le beef like never before. Sure ya coulda fried an egg on my groins right ler. Sure thon wee lawd was teasin me somethin shackin, an it was only makin me want him even more. An le mad thing was, my charms usually woulda worked by len. I just coulden put my finger on why he hadn't succumbed til my 'buck-me' eyes. But while I was day-dreamin about Sexy Anthony, sure didden I hear Big Sally-Ann at le door, wailin. Sure, I heard her comin from le tap a le street til be hanast. She was pure wailin like a banshee. An here's me til myself, oh, here's le start of it nie.

Well. After I let her in, she was hysterical. Sure Igor still hadn't rang or text, an she was startin til think he was either dead or had bucked somebady else.

Here's me, 'Whhhaaaaaaa? No way, chum. He would never get anybady as good as you. Don't think lat! An he's probably nat dead, either.'

An len here bes her, 'What do ya mean "prabably nat"?'

An here bes me, 'Ack, I mean, it's nat as if he'd get run over by a truck carryin garlic an crucifixes like, is it?' Nen, I prays til God lat he hasn't been. An Big Sally-Ann lucks at me like I'm nat wise an nen sits down on le settee.

So, I gets down on my knees in front of her an here bes me, 'Nie. Hear me, Sally-Ann. I know ya love thon Igor, an ya want him here. But you were all right before you met him, weren't ya?'

An here bes her, 'A suppose, like.' An she sniffs like a wee kid after cryin ler heart out.

An here bes me, 'Nie, it's yer birthday le day. Don't be cryin over a man. It's yer duty til get blacked an have a laugh an dance til *Dirty Dancin*, all right?'

An here bes her, 'A suppose.' An nen she cracks a smile.

Nen I lucked an sure she'd run out in her three-quarter length 'Hello Kitty' jammie battams, an le legs were like a footballer's. Here's me, 'Sure ya could use thon legs til sweep le floor! Ya can't wear a ballerina dress wih legs like thon! Nie, away an get thon hair washed, an get thon legs shaved an all.'

An nen she busts out laughin an here bes her, 'Ack, Titty's gonna wax lem for me later lis mornin.'

An here bes me, 'Right, will. Lat's more like it. Nie, mon we'll have a birthday brekkie … A feg, a gravy ring, a cuppa tea an *Jeremy Kyle*, an nen it's off til Titty's til get defuzzed an glammed up.'

An here bes her, 'Awye will!' An sure she's pure excited again. An sure I was chompin at le bit til get rid a her, so I could start wih my birthday preparations an all. So after King Kyle, she threw on my leopard print housecoat an dandered back up home til get a bath. I said I'd see her later on, cos I was busy wih le decorations. So, I quickly tuck a luck at my til-do list an len rung Sinead til see hie le decorations were comin on. Sure she telled me lat Donna had nabbed some balloons from le funeral do already, an le christenin do was in next so all was in hand.

Sinead was takin a trip down til le swimmers for a sneaky buck in le storeroom wih Gorgiz Gavin again, so she said she'd meet me up at le shebeen about three a'clack wih le balloons an all, an lat Sexy Anthony would be bringin her. So sure lat was like a firework goin off in my minge so it was, I was delighted. So, I decided til get all my bits done early, so I could dickey myself up for Sexy Anthony. Like all I would need was for him til drink a couple a cacktails an once he was tipsy, I could malest him. Simples, like.

So, I says til myself, right, I need til get lem strawberries squashed. So, I stomped round til my ma's house, because she had welly boots an a bucket. Sure, I'd seen it done on TV one day – I'd lost le remote control, an was hung over til fuck, an sure I coulden be arsed gettin off le settee til change le channel, so I had til watch a dacumentary about makin wine. Sure ley were trampin on grapes an all an it lucked like a pure geg like. So I was champin at le bit til have a go at it.

16

Cat-piss Dackries

Well. On le way til my ma's house, didden I bump intil Big Billy Scriven. He had two blue begs an here bes me til him, 'You on le drink already, chum?' An I was still a bit pissed off wih him like, cos it was his fault really lat I missed out on le strawberries.

An here bes him, 'No, Maggie. I managed til get some more strawberries for ya. Nicked lem from a delivery van outside le Co-Ap lis mornin.' An right enough, ler was about six baxes a strawberries in each beg.

Here's me, 'Whhhhhhhhhhhaaaaaaaaaaaa? You'll go til any lengths til get yer hole chum, but nie I'm nat pramisin anything, ya hear?' An he grins like he knows I'm a cert, an sure I thinks about Sexy Anthony an his tight T-shirt an all lem ripples down le front of it, an his tan an his wee tight arse an sure I was drippin. So, I trailed Big Billy intil an entry, an he bucked me up le back door a Janny Milligan's house. Sure Janny's dog was goin buck daft in le back yard listenin til us, an I was afeared a him comin out thinkin he was gettin robbed like, but it didden stap me. Sure I was like a dog on heat myself.

Anyhie, after lat, Big Billy winked at me an here bes him, 'See ya le night, ya big ride, ye.' An here bes me til myself, nat if I see ya first, cos I'll be buckin thon stud Sexy Anthony. Nen I felt a bit guilty about Big Billy, but sure I knew he would find somebady else til buck an it woulden be a prablam. Like it wassen as if we were a couple nor nathin. We both knew where we stood.

So, when I gat til my ma's, she was sittin in le armchair wih her wellies on, smokin a feg. Ler was two buckets sittin on le floor beside her, an she was all excited an all. Here bes her, 'Where le frig have ya been, I've been waitin ages on ya gettin here.'

An here bes me, 'Ack, I was talkin til Big Billy

Scriven, Ma. He kept me back.'

An here bes her, 'Oh, awye? Well? Any gassip til tell?'

An here bes me, 'No. We're just friends, lat's all.' Nen she sighs an lucks down at her boots. An nen here bes me, 'Ack in le name a God, Ma – what have ye on yer kebs like?' Sure she had childer's welly boots on, pink wih wee cartoon pigs drew on.

An here bes her, 'Ack, sure ley were le only ones I could get in my size for Christ's sake.' Sure my ma only takes a size three in a shoe. Sure she's been shrinkin since 1995, but strangely, her mouth's gat bigger. Here bes her, 'Right drap le strawberries intil one a lem buckets til I get squashin lem.' So, I drapped a few baxes a strawberries intil one a lem, an le rest intil another. An it didden luck like much. My ma says, 'Is lat it?' An nen I starts til tell her about le Lord Mayor an all an here bes her, 'Ack, he's a wee rat, him. Imagine doin lat on ye. Hie dare he! Well, I'm nat votin for him nie, like.'

An here bes me, 'People don't vote le Lord Mayor in, Ma.'

An here bes her, 'Well who voted him in len?'

An here bes me, 'Some dope, probably.'

An here bes her, 'Awye, yer right there.' Nen she stamps her foot down an squelches le strawberries, an sure she starts stampin down again an again. But as she stomped down each time, she left off a fart. Here bes me, 'Ack for le sake lat is fuck, Ma, can ya nat fart on le strawberries!'

An here bes her, 'Ack, I can't help it – wait til you're near seventy len talk til me about "stop fartin". You're lucky I'm nat fallowin through!' So, we both get til work stampin on le strawberries but sure once ley had started til go til mush, ley had shrunk even more, an ler was hardly anythin in le buckets. It would only make a few dackries an sure I was heartbroken.

So, I went out til le yard til smoke a feg an have a think. Sure ler was bound til be somewhere lat I could buy more strawberries. So, I was thinkin an thinkin an puffin an puffin when I hears an almighty shriek an yell, an I think my Ma's tuck a heart attack wih all lat stampin. Either lat or she has actually fallowed through. But when I run in, sure she was standin beside le buckets, an her cat was pissin over le tap a lem. Well. I actually had like a meltdown. Sure, I chased le cat an it went squealin out til le yard, so I chased it down le entry, callin it every name under le sun. Nen I chased it across le road, an I was prayin for a bin lorry til come an squash le wee shit. I've never liked lat cat. Sure it won't even let ya stroke it, it bites ya. Ratten wee shite, I bet it pissed on le strawberries on purpose. So, when it disappeared through a hedge, an I coulden chase it no more, I bolted down til Big Billy Scriven's flat til take it out on him. Sure he answered le door in his Y-fronts an when he saw le luck in my eye, he run back intil le flat an I run after him, whackin his arse. Here bes me, 'My ma's cat's fuckin pished on le strawberries – nie we've none! Lis is all yer fault – why coulden ye have telled thon Lord Mayor ley were sold. Or brought lem out til me before he came!' Nen I tuck my welly boot off an flung it at him, but he ducked an it hit le wall, leavin a splat a strawberry juice before it fell til le floor.

Nen I just breaks down an pure cries! An like, I never cry. Only when ley reduced le Bru lat time, an lat other time when I drapped my fegs down a drain when I was buckin Big Billy at le bus shelter. But sure Big Billy came over an put his arm around me an says, 'No point cryin over squashed strawberries, Maggie.'

An here bes me, 'Ano. But it's nat just lat.' Nen I starts til tell him all about Big Sally-Ann an hie she was leavin me for Igor, an lat everything's changed an all. But he just tells me I'm bein daft an til catch myself on.

Here bes him, 'Yous two are le terrible twosome! Yez are never gonna get split up for fuck's sake!' Nen I thinks til myself, ack, he's right like. So, I pulls myself tilgether an he says he will get til work again on findin more strawberries. So, I dander back down til my ma's house an sure she is scrapin le dregs of le squashed strawberries off her boots intil a bowl. An here bes me, 'Ack Ma, ler's nat enough ler for dackries, forget it.'

So, I saunters back down til le flat til crack on wih my list. Well. Sure I had a cup a tea an a feg an here's me til myself, le only things left til do are til put le decorations up an get le glitterball thing from le Stadium. So, I trats back up til le Stadium an Wee Sandra on le reception goes til get it for me. Sure I had asked her for it le week before at le corner bar an she'd said, 'Awye, no prabs. Anythin for Big Sally-Ann's party like.' Sure Big Sally-Ann was well loved up an down le Road. She was like a wee mini national treasure. So, Wee Sandra gat me le ball an I tuck it back home. Nen here's me til myself, right, time til get myself luckin like a big ride. So, I goes til have a bath. Sure, I scrubbed an rubbed an lathered an rinsed. Sure I'd never had a bath like it in my life. I was lat tired from all le washin an le stress of le day, sure I fell asleep in it.

Well, I woke up til hear bangin on le front door an here's me til myself, 'Whhhhaaaaaaaaaaaaaa?' Sure, I jumped outta le bath an run til le door ballik naked. I lucked through le letter bax, an ler was Sinead an Sexy Anthony behind her, holdin about fifty balloons on strings. Sure I near died. I had no make-up on nor nathin.

Here bes me, 'Frig what time is it?'

An here bes Sinead, 'It's four a'clack Maggie, I've been ringin yer mobile, hope ye're nat buckin somebady in ler!' Nen she lets out a laugh an Sexy Anthony tuts. Nen I thinks til myself, frig, if it hadda just been Sexy Anthony by himself, I coulda shoved a diddy through le letter bax til get him in le mood before I malested him. But, instead, I run til le airin cupboard an trailed out a towel. Nen I wrapped it round me an went til let lem in. Sure I was pure skundered lat Sexy Anthony would see me wih no make-up on like.

Sinead bounced in first an here bes her, 'Fuck a duck Maggie are ya nat even ready yet? We've til get lese decorations an all up – Anthony's gonna give us a hand.'

An here bes Sexy Anthony, 'As long as yez are quick like.'

An here bes me til him, 'I can be quick, chum.' Nen I bats my eyelids at him, but he just lucks at le wall. So, I says, 'Right, gimme five mins til I shove somethin on,' an I runs til le bedroom. An just as I was about til go through le door, Sinead says, 'Maggie?'

An I turns round an here's me, 'Whaaaaaaa?' An here bes her, 'Yev a hole in yer towel like, at le arse.' An sure enough, ler was a hole in it just le size a my arse.

So here bes me, 'Well, if yev gat it, flaunt it,' an I dandered back intil my bedroom, swingin my hips like a catwalk madal. An here's me til

myself, oh yer man will have a semi all right nie.
Wait til I get le houl a him later on …

17

Buckey-Ar-La

Well, I shoved on my yella neon leggins an my black off-the-shoulder belly tap an away we went up til decorate le shebeen. Sure, when we gat ler, Wee Myrtle, le auld doll lat runs le bar, had put up Christmas decorations an all for us. Ler was Christmas lights all around le room an tinsel around le chairs. Ya could hardly smell le spilt beer lat was festerin in le carpet, or le whiff a pish from le bogs at all. It was, like, perfect. So, we put up le photies lat we'd capied, an set le balloons around le place. Len, I gat up on a chair til fix le glitter ball til le ceilin. Sure, while Sinead was puttin some pictures up in le bogs, I gat Sexy Anthony til come an hold le chair for me while I stood on it. Well, I thinks til myself, seize le moment an all lat. So sure, didden I whip my bra up an released le baps, an when I stretched up til le ceilin, ley were hangin outta le battam of le belly tap.

Nen I says, 'Anthony, does lis luck all right til you?' An sure he lucks up an near gets a diddy in his eye.

Here bes him, 'Aye, it's all right. But ya might wanna adjust yer tap, luv.'

Nen I titters an here bes me, 'Oh, silly me.' So, I pulls my bra back down an steps down an sure I'm eye til eye wih him an here bes me, 'Ler's plenty more where lat came from, chum.' Nen he just lucks at me like I'm nat wise. So sure, I start til feel panicky again an I didden know what til say an sure I tuck a pure beamer an here's me til myself, what is lis wee lawd doin til me? I can't even flirt wih him – I go til bits!

So sure, don't I make a pure dick outta myself again an start swayin on le spat singin, 'Sexy. Everythin about ya's so sexy. You don't even know what ya ga-at. Ya really hit my spa-hat. Oh yeah.' Nen I grabs my cratch like Michael Jackson an dummy bucks my hand. But ler's just no reaction from Sexy Anthony. Nen I was just about til throw him on le floor an sit on his face when Sinead comes outta le bogs an says, 'Right, lat's us done. Donna did good, didden she? She's dead excited about comin le night too.'

An here's me, 'Awye.' Nen we all goes out til le car an le journey home is dead quiet. Nen I thinks, maybe Sexy Anthony has finally gat it – I'm after him. But when ley drap me off, he hardly lucks at me.

But I didden have much time til sit an think about it. Because Big Sally-Ann an Will arrived. Sure she had her make-up done an her legs smooth an she was ready til start gettin blacked. Will was carryin about a tonne a Buckey an a couple a battles a peach Cancorde too. Here's me, 'Whaaaaaaaaaaaaaaa? We're gonna get pure stocious le night chummers!' An I was dead excited til see Big Sally-Ann's face when she seen le shebeen an all. She was luckin le part like – sure Titty had curled her hair an all an she was brill luckin. But sure I hadn't even an eyelash on me, so I started til get ready, while she telled me all about her pamperin an Will gat til makin us cacktails made outta Buckey, Cancorde an Coke.

Sure Titty coulden wax Big Sally-Ann's legs in le end cos ley were just too bushy. So, she had til barra her da's electric shaver til get le bulk of it off. Nen Titty gat carried away an tried til give her a Brazilian. But ley coulden get le sides even so in le end, le lat came off. Here's me, 'Whaaaaaaaaaaaaaaaa? Are you tellin me ye've a baldy fanny? Sure you'll be freezin! Nat til mention, what will Igor think? Sure he's used til hairy armpits an a three a'clack shadda on his women, never mind a baldy twat!'

An Big Sally-Ann just sighed an here bes her, 'Ack, I've resigned myself til le fact he's nat comin, Maggie.' Nen she slumps down in le chair an starts gluggin from a battle of Buckey.

An here bes me, 'Ack, ya never know. He might turn up at le last minute like in le films.' An Big Sally-Ann nods but I know she doesen believe it. An nen I thinks til myself, like ano I've wished le wee frigger dead, but like I didden really mean it. But when I get a houl of le wee cont lat gat Igor lifted an deported, I'm gonna knack ten bells outta lem. Well, wee Will came intil le livin room an here bes him, 'Put thon battle down for frig's sake Sally-Ann. We is

124

classy bitches le night – check out lese bad boys!' An sure he has a tray wih three cacktails on it wih wee umbrellas an slices a lemon on le sides an all.

Here's me, 'Whaaaaaaaaaaaaaaaaaaaaa?'

An lis is him, 'Oh awye, Maggie. Get yer lips round lat!'

An here's me, 'What's it called?'

An here bes Will, 'It's called a Muff Guzzler – cos they're dark, mysterious an will do yer head in in le mornin!' An sure I wallaped him round le head wih my slipper. But I tuck a sip an sure it tasted like tar, so I lit a feg till drown out le taste an carried on. Big Sally-Ann was still a bit down about Igor nat showin up, but she was takin le drink an I thinks, le sooner she gets blacked, le sooner she'll stap thinkin about Igor.

So, we start playin thon drinkin game where you put le word 'cont' in place of a word from a film title, and after about ten minutes of lat, Big Sally-Ann is laughin her head off an Igor's forgatten. Nen here bes me, 'Right, my turn til make le cacktails.' So, I sauntered intil le kitchen an started til make a concaction. I poured Buckey, vadki, Lucozade and limeade intil a jug and stirred it round. It ended up a dark murky green colour an here bes me til myself, perfect! So, I poured out three glasses an tuck lem intil Big Sally-Ann an Will. Here bes Will, 'What le fuck's lat? It lucks like swamp water?'

An here bes me, 'Lis, my friends, is called a "Buckey-Ar-La" – made in hanar of our wee friends from le other road lat have helped us wih le birthday organisations an all.'

Nen here bes Big Sally-Ann, 'A Buckey-Ar-La – lat's quality like!' Nen she tuck a sip an started coughin, 'Fuck me Maggie, lat would singe yer eyebrows and put hairs on your chest luv!'

Nen here bes me, 'But it gets ya blacked like! Down em!'

So sure, we all downed le Buckey-Ar-Las an in lat minute, we were all pished. Here bes me, 'Ack, I love it when a plan comes tilgether!'

Nen here bes Will, in his best Mr T voice, 'You damn fool!'

An we all piss ourselves laughin. Nen I thinks til myself, frig, I may finish gettin ready, because if I drink any more of lem Buckey-Ar-Las, I'll end up jivin wih Sexy Anthony in my housecoat an slippers! I hadn't even gat my fake tan on an it was ten a'clack. So, we started til get le glad-rags on. Will had a lovely black shirt on lat shimmered an black trousers an here bes me til him, 'Yer luckin lush, big lawd!'

An here bes him, 'I'm dyin for a lumber le night, like.'

An nen in comes Big Sally-Ann. Sure she was gorgeous. I was a bit teary. Here bes me, 'Ack, love!'

An here bes her, 'Ano!'

An here bes Will, 'Proud a ye big sis!' An sure we had a big group hug.

Nen, I disappeared intil le bedroom til get my frock on. Sure it was a black dress – skin tight wih sequins all over it. I nicked it from lat wee shap 'Quiz' at le Abbeycentre an had kept it especially for lat night. Sure I was sparklin like a rackstar when I rolled intil le livin room. Here bes Will, 'Fuck me, I think I've turned straight.'

An here bes Big Sally-Ann, 'Frig, Sexy Anthony won't know what hit him le night!' An me an Will did wee twirls for her. So, we downed le lat of our cacktails an tuck a battle a peach Cancorde each for le walk up til le shebeen. Sure we were gettin horns beeped at us an all walkin up le Road an we were pure lovin it.

18

Better le Dick Ya Know Lan le Dick Ya Don't

Well, we walked intil le shebeen an sure ler was a good wee crowd ler already. I tuck a luck at Big Sally-Ann an sure her mouth was hangin open an here's her, 'Whaaaaaaaa? Maggie, did you do all lis for me?'

An here's me, 'Awye. Course I did! See le photies?' An sure she walks around le room pure delighted at le decorations an all. She spies le ones of us on le Twelfth Day, standin at le bandstand listenin til le speeches an here bes her, 'WE. LOVE. LE. REV. I.P!' an here bes me, 'ULSTER SAYS MUFF!' an nen we both bust out laughin rememberin it all.

Nen here bes her, 'Frig Maggie, we've had some gegs over le years, haven't we?'

Nen here bes me, 'We sure have, mucker.'

Len she spats le glitter ball an here bes her, 'Just like in le film! Oh lis is like le best birthday like ever! You're le bestest chum in le world!'

So, we goes up til le bar an I'm about til tell her about le strawberry dackrie fiasco, when I hear somebady callin my name from le door. So, I turns round an sure it's Big Billy Scriven. Here's me, 'Ack, what is it?' An he tells me til come outside. So, here's me til myself, if he's luckin a jump out le back, I'm sayin 'no' cos I want le Muff fresh for Sexy Anthony. So, I goes out an sure he's standin ler in le dark wih two armfuls of big green things.

Here's me, 'Whaaaaaaaaaa?'

An here bes him, 'I carried lese watermelons.'

An here's me, 'Whhhhhhhaaaaaa?'

An here's him, 'I coulden get strawberries. But I could get watermelons. What about watermelon dackries? Sure ley are red inside – who's gonna know le difference? Everybady's blacked already, an ley are easy til squash – luck.' An he nods down at a big basin on le ground, full of squashed watermelons.

Here's me, 'Billy yer a friggin genius wee lawd!' So, I shouts intil Big Sally-Ann, 'I'll be back in ten minutes chum!' An she laughs an nods an I'm thinkin, she thinks I'm away til buck Big Billy! An I laughs. But, sure, she was right, because me an him gat intil le basin til squash le watermelons an sure we had til do it bare foot. An sure, we ended up havin a touchey-feeley-no-putty-inny while stompin on le watermelons, an sure all lat red juice squelchin in between my toes was givin me le horn, sure, I coulden take no more, so I let him fling me over a beer barrel an whack one intil me.

Well, by le time we gat back intil le shebeen, it had filled up rightly. Le auld dolls from le Mountainview Darts Team was ler, all le regulars, I seen Jake-Le-Peg at le bar drinkin a pint an Big Sally-Ann was sittin wih Will, drinkin what was left of le Cancorde. So, I runs behind le bar an starts mixin le watermelon slush wih vadki an len I tells Wee Myrtle what til do til finish off le cacktails. So, I goes an gets Big Sally-Ann an tells her I've a surprise for her. So sure, I puts my hands round her eyes an leads her up til le bar an Wee Myrtle has a line a watermelon dackries waitin for us.

Here bes Big Sally-Ann, 'Whaaaaaaa? Strawberry dackries! From Benidorm. Oh, Maggie, ye've thought of everything! You are le bestest chum in le world. I pure love ya like!' An nen she gives me le biggest bear hug ever. So, we gets some of lem down us, an I tells her le story about le strawberries an le watermelons an she pure pishes herself.

Nen here bes her, 'Luck at le trouble ye've went til for all lis, Maggie. I pure can't believe it like.' Nen I goes til hug her back, an I sees somethin outta le corner of my eye lat freezes me. Sure, ler, standin behind Big Sally-Ann, is Thelma, le hermaphrodite.

Sure I clenches my fist til take a swing at her when here bes her, 'Wait, wait, Maggie. I've somethin til say.'

An Big Sally-Ann turns round an says, 'Nie, nie, I don't want any fightin on my birthday night. Nat until I've done my dance, anyhie.'

An Big Thelma lucks terrified an here bes her, 'Ack Sally-Ann, I'm sarry what I did til ya. An ler's somethin else … it was me lat rung le caps on Igor.'

Here's me an Big Sally-Ann tilgether, 'Whaaaaaaaaaaaa?'

An lis is her, 'Awye. I'm awful sarry. I was an awful woman. Awful. I coulda killed dead things a few weeks ago. Til I started my HRT. Sure my hormones were haywire, I'm tellin ya I didden know if I was comin or goin. Len it all kicked in what I'd done, an I seen Sally-Ann goin about wih a face on her like a well-skelped arse, an I felt terrible.'

Here bes me, 'You're gonna feel terrible in le Mater chum when I've broke yer neck!' An I goes til lunge at her, but Big Sally-Ann holds me back.

Here bes her, 'Maggie. Don't. She's sarry, luck at her.' Nen I lucks an Thelma's all big eyes an battam lip an here bes Big Sally-Ann, 'Remember le time before my ma went on le HRT? Sure she tried til strangle my da wih a pair a my fishnet tights.'

An here's me, 'Awye, I remember lat night well.' Sure Big Doris had tried til strangle him, right enough. An len, when we wrestled le tights off her, she started batein him round le head wih his own false leg. Sure it was a pure murder picture. Le dacter had til be rung til come an give her an injection of somethin til calm her down. It was terrible.

So, here's me, 'Well, I suppose fair play til ya for comin an tellin us. At least nie we know who done it.'

An here bes Big Sally-Ann, 'Awye. Doesen change le fact lat he's nat here, like.' Nen Big Thelma says sarry again an Big Sally-Ann tells her til get a watermelon dackrie down her neck an til forget about it.

An here bes me, 'You have a heart a gold chum. If lat was me, I'd have bust her bake for her.' An Big Sally-Ann just nods an len Big Dave-Le-Rave, le DJ, tells us lat he's gonna play our song next. So, Big Sally-Ann goes for a pish, just as Sinead, Donna an Sexy Anthony come in. But sure, I coulden get over til lem because Big Billy Scriven had gat le houl of me an was trailin me intil a corner.

Here bes me, 'You're like a dog on heat le day, chum. I wonder would ya ever?'

An here bes him, 'I wanted til give ya somethin.'

An here bes me, 'What is it? A sausage

surprise? Or a cheeky diddy grope? Whaaaaaaaa?'

An nen he pulls out a big bax an says, 'Lis.'

An here bes me, 'Whaaaaaaaa?' So, I pulls off le lid an sure I near died. It was a pair a red, sparkly peep-toe shoes. Just like le ones lat I'd seen in thon shap, Big Girl. I lucked at Big Billy an he smiled an sure my groins went buck daft.

Here bes me, 'Hie did ya know about lem shoes?'

An here bes him, 'Ack, ya were goin on about lem one day at my flat an I says til myself, ack, I'll go down an get lem for her.'

An here bes me, 'Le way til a woman's heart is through shoes, chum. An tell me, did ya really pay an extra fifty quid for Big Sally-Ann's fake passport? You must pure love her.'

An here bes him, 'Nat her, ya dope, you!'

An sure I lumbered le bake pure off him. But len, as I was doin a bidda tonsil ticklin wih Big Billy, I lucks over his shoulder an sees Sinead, Donna an Sexy Anthony sittin down wih Will an here's me, oh frig, Sexy Anthony's luckin buckable all right. Sure he had tight jeans an a white shirt on, open at le chest an ya could just see le start a his pecs. He was gettin wired in til

135

le cacktails an he lucked all smiley an relaxed for a change. Here's me til myself, frig he is, like, le biggest ride in le world. An like, I was pure torn. Like Big Billy had gat me shoes an helped me wih le watermelons an all. An he had dickied himself up a bit for le big birthday do. But Sexy Anthony was like some kinda male madal, an I pure wanted him! But len I remembered thon buck eejit Mr Red White an Blue an hie I had le severe sweats for him. An he turned out til be a woman bater an a dwarf bucker! So, I wonders if it's better le dick ya know, lan le dick ya don't …

But before I could do anythin else, Dave-Le-Rave stapped le music an announced lat me an Big Sally-Ann was about til do le dance. So, I started til walk til le dancefloor an Big Sally-Ann bounced outta le bogs an we met in le middle.

Here bes me til her, 'Are ya ready, chum?'

An here bes her, 'Ready as I'll ever be, chum.' Nen Wee Myrtle flicks le lights down low an everybady hushes, well nearly everybady. We heard some commotion at le front door an turned round an sure ler he was. Like yer man from *An Officer an a Gentleman* standin in le doorway. Big Igor.

19

Le Time of My Life

Well. Big Sally-Ann let a squeal outta her an run til le doorway, leavin me standin on le middle of le dancefloor like a right knob. Sure she was huggin an kissin him, an he was throwin her up in le air an twirlin her round. An here's me til myself, fuckin great. So, I slunk off le dancefloor over til le table where Will, Sinead, Donna an Sexy Anthony was sittin.

Here bes Sinead, 'He made it, len.'

An here bes me, 'Awye. In le nick a time. Sure it's all good.' But inside, my heart was broke about it an I was prayin lat le glitterball would fall from le ceilin an cave his head in.

Big Sally-Ann waved at me an pointed at Igor an I give her a thumbs up, an my bestest fake smile. Nen ley both tratted til le dancefloor, an tuck ler positions. I smiled at le big girl, an she smiled back. Len she pointed out le photies on le wall til Igor, an le glitterball, an le watermelon dackries. An he was smilin too, an len she whispered in his ear an he was noddin an all, an Dave-Le-Rave was just startin til play, 'Le Time a My Life', when Big Sally-Ann yells, 'Stap! Wait a minute!' So, Dave-Le-Rave mumbled somethin lat sounded like 'buck-eejit', an Big Sally-Ann kissed Igor an he went til le bar. Nen she lucks at me, an starts til walk over. Here's me til myself, what le frig's goin on nie. Nen she comes over til le table, takes my hand an says, 'Nobady puts Maggie in le corner.'

Here's me, 'Whaaaaaaaaaaaaa?'

An here bes her, 'Luck at what ye've done for me, all le organisin, gettin me outta jail, le surprises an all – ler's no way I'm nat doin lis dance wih you, my wee mucker.'

An here's me, 'Go on ya sentimental auld shite ye!' But sure I was pure delighted! I shoved my new red sparkly shoes on, an we skipped til le dancefloor as Dave-Le-Rave started le song.

Well, we tuck hands an here bes Big Sally-Ann

til me, 'Come on spaghetti arms, gimme some tension, ya ballbeg!'

So, here bes me, 'Stay in yer bax an don't come in mine.'

Nen here bes her, 'Woulden touch yer bax wih a ten-foot bargepole chum. God knows where it's been!'

Nen here bes me, 'Ack, fuck off you!' Nen we both giggles an le music starts. Well, we started til do le forward an back steps like Janny an Baby, an le crowd started til clap along wih le music. Like Big Sally-Ann wassen as stressed out as I thought she'd be. Big Igor turnin up had calmed her down about it all. Le crowd loved us like. Ley were cheerin an wolf-whistlin, an Big Sally-Ann was as happy as a pig in shite. We gat all le moves right, an were lovin every minute of it. Len, after I had flung Big Sally-Ann around a bit more, it was time for le lift. Sinead tuck her position behind me an Big Sally-Ann tuck a run at us an away she went, up intil le air. Sinead grabbed her shoulders an I had her hips an we held her up high. Le crowd let a 'whoop' out as Big Sally-Ann balanced on our hands. Sure it was amazeballs, like. Le glitterball was twinklin specks of light all around all le shacked faces as we held Big Sally-Ann steady.

Nen Big Sally-Ann shouts, 'Yeeeoooww-wwww. Get it inda ye!' I lucked over at le bar an Big Igor was clappin an shoutin, 'Yeeha! Yeeha!' Big Billy Scriven was downin dackries an everybady at our table was clappin an cheerin us on too. Thelma le hermaphrodite was cryin intil her hands an I thinks til myself, ack, she's still nat right, like – maybe she needs a patch on or somethin.

Len, we put Big Sally-Ann back down on til le floor an Sinead went back til le table. I started til twirl her around an nen she twirled me around an sure I was pure delighted til be le one til do le dance. Nen, as le song started til come til le end, Big Igor came on til le dancefloor. I gave him Big Sally-Ann's hand, like a father givin his daughter away at her weddin. An he led her around le floor for le end of le song. Sure ley were naturals tilgether like. She was like a wee wispy fairy in his big arms. An I was happy for her. An I says til myself, Ack, good luck til lem. As long as we can still have a laugh an get blacked tilgether, I can share her wih him, if it makes her happy.

So, I waltzed over til le table. An stapped dead in my tracks. Sure Sexy Anthony was lumberin le bake off our Will!

Here's me til Sinead, 'What le Scooby Doo is goin on here?'

An here bes her, 'Ack, did ya nat know our Anthony was gay? I thought I told ya?' An here bes me, 'Ah, I don't think ya did, chum! Sure he has pictures of half-naked women all over his bedroom walls!'

Nen here bes her, 'Ack, ley are for my ma's benefit. Sure if she found out he was a bumder, she'd have Father Paul down doin an exorcism on him or sendin him off til Maynooth til join le priesthood!' Sure I tuck a pure beamer at all le times I had tried til seduce him an he was havin none of it. Sure I had dry bucked my own hand earlier on lat day, an flashed him my diddies an all. An don't even remind me about singin 'Doncha' til him! An all along, he batted for le other team. Like I coulden believe I had missed it. It seemed abvious once she'd told me. It musta been le runnin about wih Big Sally-Ann an all le buckin wih Big Billy an Jake-Le-Peg lat had affected my gay-dar.

But here, I kinda thought, well, at least nie I know lat le Muffsta charm hasn't died. Like, I was startin til seriously doubt myself for a wee while ler. But it wassen me at all – it was him! Sure ya can take le bender til le furry cup, but ya can't make him drink. So, in lat minute, I gat my confidence back. An I tuck a luck around le room. Donna was at le bar wih her hand down Jake-Le-Peg's Kappa battams, an here's me, nie, lem two were made for each other – I could just imagine ler canversations about *Star Wars* an lem goin down til le shaps til get 20p frozens tilgether an all. Good luck til lem. Nen, I sees Big Thelma, le hermaphrodite, shimmyin up against Big Dave-Le-Rave an I says til myself, frig thon HRT has done thon girl wonders. Sure her moustache was away, an le lipstick was on, an here's me, ack, fair play til her too. Sinead was in le corner, slow dancin wih Big Sammy Harrison from le estate. An he must be le most wanted ride up and down le Road like. Sure he was just outta le army an was luckin hat! Everybady was after him. A big baxer wih dark hair an a smile lat would melt le girdle off yer granny. A big buckasaurus-rex he was. Here bes me til myself, fuck sake she must be wearin 'Eau de TWAT' perfume or somethin. Sure le men were drappin like flies around her. An she had sure gat le taste for a bidda orange schlong like. Here bes me, thon wee girl's doin her bit for cross-border relations single-handedly for fuck's sake! They should put her up in Stormont til sort le lat of lem out. Teach lem a trick or two. Len again, could ya imagine Bairbre de Brún an Nigel Dodds' lovechild? Boke. Maybe nat …

I tuck a watermelon dackrie off le table an downed it in one go. Sure my gob, throat an gullet was frozen wih all le ice Wee Myrtle had put in it. Wee frigger was chargin three pound for lem – always on le luck-out til make a buck. Len, I feels two warm hands round my hips, an I knew whose ley were. I started til swing my hips left an right an len back an forward, I heard him snigger intil my ear, len kiss it. I twirled around, just as Dave-Le-Rave had started til play 'I've Had le Time of My Life' again.

Here bes Dave, 'Everybady up! Lis is le last time I'm playin lis shite le night, len it's back til Scooter an "Castles in le Sky".' So, everybady bolted til le dancefloor til do some seriously dirty dancin. We're talkin semis an dry-buckin like. Big Billy pulled me towards him, so we were groin til groin, an here bes him, 'Maggie, yer luckin well le night. Sure I could take ya home nie an buck ya til le cows come home.'

An here bes me, 'But sure I love lis song!' An I pulls him on til le dancefloor wih everybady else. Like, he had scrubbed up well. He'd gat his hair cut so it didn't luck like a burnt-out bird's nest no more. He'd left his Fila tracksuit at home an had a pair of Evisu jeans on wih a dark grey shimmery shirt on tap. It lucked a bit 80s retro like an le jeans were defo a capy – prabably from le Sunday market. But it wassen a bad effort.

So, I starts til sing it til him. Here bes me,

Nie, I've had le time of my life,
Nie I know I've bucked ye loads before,
It's so true,
But I've gat a request for you …
I've been waitin for so long,
For a man til come along,
An bum-ride me.
So I'm givin you le nod,

Cos le night yer gonna prod … yer fantasy!
Nie wih water in my eyes,
I'm gonna give you a fleshy prize,
Ride le arse of me!
So, get some Vaseline in yer hand,
Lube me up, if you understand,
Make me super sli-deee.
Just remember,
Get me something,
Lat I can bite down hard on,
Thank God yer hung like a frog,
An nat fuckin King Kong!
Beeee-cause …
I'm havin le ride of my life,
No I've never done lis shit before,
Well, maybe once or two …
But lat was well before I met you.

Well, lat seemed til wind him up like a
spring. Because Big Billy whisked me up off le
dancefloor, an flung me over his shoulder, like
a sack a spuds. Nen, he started til carry me
towards le door.

Nen here bes me til him, 'Billy! Billy! I have til
stay til le end for Big Sally-Ann! She's only forty

once, ya know. An we are muckers for life!' Like, I was rightly like wih le Buckey an le Cancorde, but I was luckin til get absolutely blacked after le stressful week lat I'd had. An besides lat, I really wanted til see Big Sally-Ann shit-faced an havin 'le time of her life' an all. Like, men come an go, don't ley? But yer chums are priceless, like I always say, chums are thicker lan water. An no matter who came on le scene, I knew lat ley woulden break me an Big Sally-Ann apart.

So, Big Billy tuck me over til le bar an we gat a tray a cacktails til bring over til le table. An nen all le gang was ler. Me an Big Billy, Big Sally-Ann an Igor, Sinead an Big Sammy Harrison, our Will an Sexy Anthony an Donna an Jake-Le-Peg. Big Igor was tellin us all hie he'd lost his phone when he was pickin mushrooms in Transylvania an Big Sally-Ann was hangin on his every word. Nen just as I was luckin at le big girl, a wee tear came til my eye an she lucked at me an smiled.

Nen here bes her, 'Thank you for bein a friend.'

Nen I sings, 'Travelled down le road an back again.'

Nen she sings, 'Your heart is true – you're a

pal an a confidant.'

Nen sure, I gets carried away an stands up an belts out, 'I'm not ashamed til say, I hope it always will stay this way, My hat is off, won't you stand up and take a bow.'

Nen, just as everybady thinks lat I've lost le plat, Big Sally-Ann stands up an sings like she's friggin Tina Turner on speed, 'And if you threw a party,' nen she twirls around wih her arms flung out, 'Invited everyone you knew, You would see, le biggest gift would be from me, and le card attached would say, Thank you for bein a friend, Thank you for bein a friend.'

Nen she runs over til me an gives me le biggest squeeze an here bes me, 'Watch le diddies love!' Nen everybady claps us an we feels a bit wick like.

Nen here bes Big Billy, 'Round of applause for le Golden Girls!' Nen everybady in le room claps us an sure it was pure beezer, like. So sure, we sat an drank tilgether an gat pissed an had le best laugh … like ever. Sure le craic was ninety, so it was.

The End

Well... nat quite.

Sure after le dackries had run out, we hit le vadki. Sure we were doun shats neat an all. It gat messy. Big Sally-Ann was lat blacked, she thought she was gropin Big Igor on le dancefloor, but it was really big Eleanor Martin. Sure she is a bit manly-luckin like wih her crew-cut hair an her five a'clack shadow. But like, she was wearin a peach PVC catsuit, six-inch gold platforms an bright red lipstick — like ler was no mistakin she was a woman lat night! Well. Big Eleanor threw a vadki 'n' orange over Big Sally-Ann an len I flung Big Eleanor round le dancefloor like a ragdoll. But len Big Billy Scriven tried til play le knight in shinin armour, an gat Big Eleanor in a headlack. But sure she kneed him in le balls — an sure he was howlin like a big woman lat much, lat we all ended up pissin ourselves laughin at him. But sure by le end of le night, we were all best mates again. Just another crazy night at le shebeen! Here's me, whaaaaaaaaaaaaaaaaaaaa?

Acknowledgements

I would like to thank Blackstaff Press for publishing the book, and for their continued support. I would like to thank all my mates who I have bounced ideas off and sang Maggie's songs to … (yes, I do sing them – excruciating for whoever is listening). Massive thanks to my mum for babysitting and for an honest opinion. And thanks to Gordy (Dad) because I forgot him last time. ☺

And last but not least, a zillion thanks to all of you who have read and commented on Facebook! Who would have guessed Miss Muff would have such a following! It's all down to you so thank you for the support and for coming along to all the signings and events. I really appreciate it!

Leesa xxx

THE FIRST INSTALMENT IN
MAGGIE MUFF'S ESCAPADES – AND THE
SMASH-HIT BESTSELLER

Fifty Shades
of Red White and Blue

Well. Lis is a wee story about me an Mr Red
White and Blue. Sure didden I meet him
down in le Bru on a back-til-work interview.
He was tall, dark an bucksome– an he
was gorgiz in lem chinos.

So nie if ye want a wee giggle an yer nat too
squeamish, let me tell ye all what happened –
sure ye'll nat believe it. We're talking baps,
blindfolds an a Belfast Bus Tour ye'll
never forget. Oh Mammy, don't start me!

Maggie Muff xx

Paperback
ISBN 978-0-85640-905-9
£5.99

Also available as an eBook
EPUB ISBN 978-0-85640-077-3
KINDLE ISBN 978-0-85640-082-7
£3.99

www.blackstaffpress.com
www.leesaharker.com

Fifty Shades
of Red White and Blue